MW01204146

PRAISE FOR HELEN COX'S ROMANCE BOOKS

'It was swoon-worthy as they fell in love and I sighed my approval.'

'A steamy historical romance novella that kept me turning the pages.'

'I will definitely add this author to my favourites list.'

'One heart-soaring thrill ride.'

Five star rated comments from Booksprout reviewers.

ONCE UPON A
RUGGED
KNIGHT

HELEN LOUISE COX

Published in the United Kingdom by Helen Cox Books.

Copyright © 2021 by Helen Louise Cox.

Ebook ISBN: 9781838080181
Paperback ISBN: 978-1-914238-00-0
Hardback ISBN: 978-1-914238-01-7

Other Romance Titles by Helen Louise Cox
Disarming the Wildest Warrior
Surrendering to the Gentleman Pirate
Swept Away by the Merman

HISTORICAL NOTES

his story is deliberately set at a time in which the Great Vowel Shift was already well under way in England. This creative choice was made in order to give my two central characters at least a fighting chance of understanding each other. Major changes in the pronunciation of vowel sounds took place between 1400 and 1700 but were particularly concentrated in the 15th and 16th Centuries when spelling began to be standardised. Thus, though there would be inevitable differences between Maddie and Sir Pierce Carlyle's speech patterns, they would, so far as my research shows, recognise that they were both speaking the English language.

With regards to dialect and syntax of the 1500s, I have done my best to strike a balance between authenticity and accessibility for the modern-day reader. I have therefore peppered the story with words and sentence constructions that would have been favoured at the time Sir Pierce Carlyle lived in order to offer a flavour of the period. Given the light-hearted, nay, frivolous nature of the tale you are about to read, this seemed the most sensible course to take.

Robin Hood is mentioned briefly in this story due to the bulk of the action being set in Sherwood Forest. By the 1500s many ballads had been written about this folktale hero. Consequently, although Maddie and Sir Pierce lived almost five hundred years apart, this is one pop-culture reference that they would definitely both share. Unlike Mila Kunis.

NOTTINGHAM 2019

CHAPTER ONE

MADDIE

'Cross my palm with silver, young maiden, and I will tell you all about your days not yet lived.'

Maddie Dawson smiled at the woman with the wrinkled face, adorned in a robe made entirely of dark purple silk and hanging out the back of a covered wagon. Even with her maroon turban, set with a large green jewel, she was one of the less-garish vendors at the annual fairytale convention *Once Upon a Dream*.

Yes, Maddie had felt a little silly booking a ticket for a fairytale-oriented event at the age of thirty. Not to mention buying a "medieval princess" costume from eBay, complete with a pointed hennin hat. After doing little else but care for her ailing mother for the past two years however, she ultimately convinced herself she deserved a bit of fun. Reading fairytale stories had been the only salve for all the pain and responsibility unexpectedly mounted on her since her mother's breast cancer diagnosis. With the convention taking place just an hour away from her hometown of Lincoln, it seemed like the perfect opportunity to indulge her need for escape.

The moment she stepped out of the May sunshine and in through the doors of the Nottinghamshire Regional Conference Hall, she forgot all of her prior self-consciousness. There were many people in attendance of her age, and older. All dressed in a mix of homemade costumes or whatever they could find in their local fancy dress shop. The air was saturated with the smell of gingerbread, stewing apples, warm pumpkin pie, and the aroma of many other fairytale-inspired foods, sold on various stalls. The enchanting atmosphere was further heightened by an inspired decorative move from the organisers who had draped the entire hall from ceiling to floor with thousands of fairy lights. They twinkled in such a way that Maddie almost believed there really was magic in the air.

'Young maiden?' The elderly woman who had addressed her before tried to re-establish her attention. Her withered hand outstretched in the hope of being crossed with the five pound fee advertised on a placard near the entrance to her wagon. According to the lettering above the fee, her name was Madame Codoni.

Maddie tucked a strand of auburn hair behind her ear and tried to think of a polite way of refusing the offer. 'I don't think great things lay in my future, sorry,' she said, turning away.

'You'd be wrong.'

Slowly, Maddie turned back to Madame Codoni who now wore a knowing smile. Something about the old woman's expression made Maddie hesitate. She had planned to join the queue to have her photograph taken with one of the handsome princes and dashing knights the event coordinators had hired but the watery glaze of the old woman's grey eyes reminded her of her mother.

Maddie shook her head, trying to shake away the thoughts along with them. She didn't want to think about that today. She had thought of little else since her mother's first operation. The doctors had done all they could and now there was nothing they could do but wait and see if the tests showed her to be in remission. After the many sacrifices Maddie had made, this was a day just for her…

Still, she couldn't say no to the fortune-teller when she reminded her so much of the person she loved most in the world.

'Alright,' Maddie said, narrowing her eyes in good humour at Madame Codoni before dropping change, to the sum of five pounds, into her still-open hand. 'But no nonsense about tall, handsome strangers, if you don't mind.'

'Had some trouble with men, have we?' Madame Codoni said, waving Maddie into her wagon, which smelled strongly of jasmine incense.

Maddie shook her head and chuckled. She wasn't giving the old woman any credit for working that out after her somewhat jaded comment.

When purchasing her convention ticket online, Maddie had clicked the all-access option, which included entrance to a special masquerade ball the organisers were holding that evening once the stall-holders had packed up for the day. Although she hadn't ruled out seducing a masked stranger that evening just for the thrill of it, she didn't intend to even exchange names with any man she might take to bed. Given how her last romantic entanglement ended, they seemed far more trouble than they were ever worth. At least for the foreseeable future.

'You tell me,' Maddie answered dryly, 'you're the all-seeing oracle.'

Madame Codoni smiled what seemed a rather sly smile and indicated Maddie should sit next to a small round table. 'We shall see, what we can see.'

Without another word, Madame Codoni seated herself opposite Maddie and whipped a length of turquoise silk off a large crystal ball which had been sitting, shrouded, on the table.

Maddie did her best not to roll her eyes as Madame Codoni stared hard into the crystal and waved her hands around it as though pulling aside a veil visible only to herself. This was even more hokey than Maddie had thought it would be.

'You've had a tough time lately,' Madame Codoni said.

'Yes,' Maddie found herself admitting; though the woman's prediction was hardly specific it felt good to at least acknowledge that fact. Up until now she'd had no choice but to put a brave face on everything. 'I suppose things have been difficult.'

'And you've braved it all with grace,' said Madame Codoni. 'But you should know there are much brighter days ahead of you. Yes, yes, yes. The happiness that has been withheld will find you.'

'Something to smile about,' Maddie said, not convinced by the old woman's declaration in the least. She probably told all of her customers that. It was, after all, what everyone wanted to hear, whether true or not.

'Oh,' said Madame Codoni. 'I see why you don't want to know about future suitors. The last one hurt you deeply, didn't he?' She lifted those grey watery eyes from the crystal ball just long enough to meet Maddie's unwavering stare.

'Yes, he did,' Maddie said, while wondering if this was the worst fiver she'd ever spent. After her comment about handsome strangers, it didn't take a genius – or a clairvoyant – to work out that she was in the process of getting over *something*.

'Don't worry. It's his loss. James'll never find another one like you. Last thing you need is someone who disappears when the going gets tough. I don't need to tell you life's no easy ride. You need a partner who's as brave as you are.'

Maddie offered a polite smile, but then, on properly digesting the woman's words, started. Frowning, she mentally combed back through her exchanges with Madame Codoni. Had she mentioned James's name? She didn't think so. She wouldn't say that little weasel's name unless it was absolutely unavoidable. But she must have. There's no other way Madame Codoni could know that detail... right?

'Oh!' said Madame Codoni, peering once again into the crystal ball. '*Here's* something that should please you.'

'What's that?' Maddie replied, her tone dubious.

'You won't find a suitor in your future. Just like you wanted.'

'What? *Never?*' Maddie spluttered, instinctively looking closer at the ball herself to see if she could make anything out. But it just looked like cloudy glass to her. 'Like, not even a couple of frogs to kiss under the mistletoe at Christmas?'

Madame Codoni laughed so hard her whole body rippled in amusement. At once, remembering herself, Maddie did what she could to look unconcerned about the woman's words. She didn't believe in this claptrap anyway. It was just supposed to be a bit of fun.

'That's not quite what I meant,' said Madame Codoni. 'You will find a suitor but not in the future, in the past.'

'A suitor in the past? You're not trying to tell me that I'm going to take back one of my exes are you?' Maddie's eyes widened at the thought. Since her first school boyfriend at the age of sixteen, the men she'd dated had only helped her discern what she *didn't* want in a potential mate. The idea that she might wind up back with one of those hopeless miscreants was not good news.

'No… not someone you've already partnered with.'

'An old school friend then?'

'No… someone you've never met before.'

'But how can they be from the past if I've never met them?'

'It's… unclear,' Madame Codoni said, though from her tone Maddie couldn't help but feel that she knew more than she was letting on. 'But you are destined to meet this person very, very soon.'

Maddie opened her mouth to ask how she could meet someone soon who was, as Madame Codoni described it, not from her future, but she thought better of it. She had humoured the old woman long enough. There were dashing knights to have selfies taken with out there, or the closest approximation she was ever likely to meet. Best to wind this up.

'Well, that's all very intriguing, thank you,' Maddie said, standing. 'I shall bear what you've said in mind.'

'Wait!' Madame Codoni said, jumping to her feet. 'Every customer gets a free cocktail.'

'Oh no, that's OK,' Maddie tried, not really in the market for whatever strange concoction someone like Madame Codoni might have cooked up.

'No, no, I insist,' she said, hobbling over to another small table further back in the wagon. It was too dark back there for Maddie to make out what the old woman was doing but she returned after a moment or two. 'It's a special family recipe. A big hit with everyone who tries it. Here, take a sip.'

Gingerly accepting the glass from the woman, Maddie did as instructed and supped half a mouthful of the strange, purple liquid. The mixture, whatever it may be, was surprisingly delicious. There were definitely elderberries in there somewhere but the rest of the ingredients remained a mystery.

'Drink up, don't be shy,' Madame Codoni pushed.

Realising that she was not going to be released from Madame Codoni's company until she did as instructed, Maddie gulped down what remained in her glass.

She noticed a strange look on Madame Codoni's face as she did so but, wanting nothing more than to be on her way, she decided to ignore it.

Maddie felt perfectly fine as she said her goodbyes, lifted her gown of green velvet and negotiated the couple of steps that led back out into the conference hall.

She even managed a few paces in the direction of the knights and princes she had been aiming for in the first place.

But she made it no further.

For then, without any warning at all, the room around her began to spin. Slowly at first but then faster and faster until she had no choice but to cling to a nearby table to remain standing.

'What's happening?' she heard herself moan out.

But there was no reply. Nobody seemed even to notice that she was in distress. The world carried on around her and the spinning of her environment only quickened until everything became a grey blur. Before she knew it she had tumbled to the wooden floor of the conference hall, and then all weight left her body. She was nowhere. Hanging in space. Out of time. In a void. Unable to feel. Unable to think. Barely able to breathe.

The next thing she truly understood was the impact of a sickening jolt and a pair of deep brown eyes staring intensely into hers.

NOTTINGHAM 1548

CHAPTER TWO

PIERCE

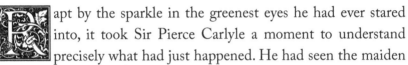

apt by the sparkle in the greenest eyes he had ever stared into, it took Sir Pierce Carlyle a moment to understand precisely what had just happened. He had seen the maiden lying in her bed of forest leaves but barely a moment before his horse would have trampled her to death. Indeed, it had felt as though she had appeared as if from nowhere. On realising the obstacle in his path, he had pulled the reins on Storm, his black steed, so hard that the beast had twisted and reared and knocked him from the saddle. From there, he had been flung and landed on top of the resting maid with force enough to shake her awake.

Forgetting the prior desperation which had sent him charging through the forest in the power of her gaze, he found himself searching for an excuse to prolong the length of time his body lay on top of hers, which was full in all the places a man would hope for. Reminding himself that his body, heart and mind were already spoken for, he cleared his throat. 'Are you hurt, my lady?' he asked, while realising he was panting. Panting? Why, he wondered, while almost at once becoming aware of how close her lips were to his. She had applied some kind of pigment to them that made them appear redder than any rose. He would have challenged any man to look at them and not consider how they might taste.

She frowned at him in such a way that he wondered if she could understand him. It was then that he noticed her hat. It looked distinctly French by design. But what would a French lady be doing out in Sherwood Forest, alone?

'Are you... fluent in English, my lady?' he said, making sure to keep his speech slow so she at least had a chance of understanding him.

'Yes,' the woman replied, her tone cautious. 'Are you..? I'm sorry, I'm a little bit... Is this... some kind of reenactment?'

Sir Pierce frowned. Her way of speaking was only just recognisable as English. Perhaps her French heritage had an impact on the way she pronounced their words. And yet, of the few Frenchmen he had met, he had never known any of them speak quite like her. 'Reenactment of what, my lady?'

'How did we get outside?' she asked, ignoring his question in a way he found somewhat impertinent. When a Knight of King Edward VI asked you a question, an answer was expected.

Reluctantly rising to his feet, Sir Pierce extended a hand to the maiden which she accepted and helped herself up.

'I will be the one to ask questions,' he said, suddenly wondering if the woman might be embroiled in some kind of sinister behaviour in the woods. Witchcraft perhaps, or thievery? The forest was known as a hideout for some truly unsavoury characters, which was perhaps why it had seemed the best place for him to flee.

'Will you indeed?' the woman replied. She seemed to have overcome her prior confusion and appeared quite amused by his words. 'I shan't argue. I find a commanding tone rather alluring on a man.'

A small, but deeply distracting smile formed on those rose red lips. For a moment, that was all Sir Pierce could focus on. But then he remembered himself, and the urgency of his ride out into the forest. If he had understood her comment correctly she was making an advance on him, and a rather forward one at that. Though not dressed in a particularly provocative manner, she must be a whore of some nature, to speak so.

'I have no time to trifle with a courtesan, lady,' he said, making sure there was a clear warning in his voice. 'Now, tell me who you are at once.'

She frowned as though his response was not as she had expected but after a few moments hesitation she answered with a small curtsey. 'Lady Madelyn Dawson, and you are?'

'Sir Pierce Carlyle. And what, pray, are you doing here alone?'

'Just out for a walk.'

'Unchaperoned?'

'Are you offering to be my chaperone, Sir Pierce?' Lady Madelyn said, that diverting smile surfacing once again.

He pushed a hand through his long, dark hair and glanced over his shoulder. No sign of Lord Holtby and his men – yet. But who knows how much of a lead he had? And in his haste to flee Sir Richard's castle there had been no time to assemble his plate armour. His breeches and his mail would offer little defence if he found himself under attack.

'Ordinarily, I would be happy to assist a maiden in need, even one as brazen as you, lady, but I haven't a moment more to spare. I must away.'

Without another word Sir Pierce re-mounted Storm, who had been huffing and stamping just a few paces away. He nudged the horse with his foot and the beast broke into a trot.

'Wait! Wait!' Lady Madelyn called after him. There was a desperate note in her voice that he could not ignore and he duly pulled at the reins, turning back in her direction.

'Is this… is this… part of the reenactment?' she said, frowning again. It seemed their exchange had proven as confusing to her as it had to him. But what was this infernal reenactment she spoke of? It dawned on Sir Pierce that the woman might be ill of mind. Leaving a vulnerable maiden in the middle of the forest alone would not normally have been something he'd even consider. But right now he had problems of his own to solve.

'I am not familiar with any reenactment, and must take my leave,' he said, making his voice as gruff as he could so that even if she were weak in the head she might understand his meaning.

'Wait, please. I know you're just trying to stay in character but I'm confused. I didn't sign up for this. I don't even know where we are. I don't recognise this forest.'

'You truly must be far from home to not know these woods, lady. This is Sherwood Forest.'

Lady Madelyn frowned. 'You mean, like the hiding place of Robin Hood? That Sherwood Forest?'

Lord, if this woman knew her geography by mere folktale, she must really be quite simple-minded. Still, Sir Pierce was not one to be cruel to people with less understanding of the world than himself. 'It is mentioned in those tales, ay my lady.'

'Something very strange is happening. I don't know how or why but –'

'There he is, murderer!' came a call in the distance. Sir Pierce started. He would recognise that voice anywhere. Lord Edmund Holtby, the true murderer who had struck last night and killed Sir Richard's brother – Lord Thomas Bentley.

'Murderer...' Lady Madelyn repeated the words, her eyes widening as she looked up at Sir Pierce with a strange mix of curiosity and uncertainty.

'And ho! He is with a fellow conspirer,' came another call.

'Fire at will!' Holtby bellowed. 'Neither foe must leave alive.'

Before Sir Pierce could blink, an arrow shot past Lady Madelyn, whipping her hair as it flew. She jumped and cried out in shock as more arrows rushed past. Lifting the shield he had stowed on the cantle of his saddle, Sir Pierce protected himself from the worst and watched in disbelief as Lady Madelyn ducked down in the grass, covering her head with her hands. That would do her no good.

Holtby's men would be upon them in moments and wouldn't think twice about killing her, or worse.

Cursing under his breath, Sir Pierce dismounted and, shielding both of them from the ceaseless onslaught of arrows, pulled her up onto his horse. She sat behind him, straddling the saddle in that ridiculous green gown that was hardly fit for riding. The second Storm was in motion she screamed and wrapped her arms tight around his torso, as though it was the first time she had ever been on a horse.

He had no time to calm her. All he could focus on was outrunning Lord Holtby and his mob before one of their arrows found its mark. Tapping Storm with his foot and jerking the reins in a manner he knew would spur his steed into a gallop, they whipped through foliage, over logs and under branches in a bid to escape while Sir Pierce tried not to get too distracted by how Lady Madelyn's body pressed so tightly against his made every last one of his senses throb.

CHAPTER THREE

addie couldn't say how long they had been riding when Sir Pierce finally slowed his horse. But she was most relieved when he did. Her years spent behind a desk in the recruitment industry hadn't exactly required any equestrian experience. The movement of the horse, alongside the disorientation of the utterly bananas situation she had somehow tumbled into, had left her feeling quite nauseated. And, if there was one thing she wasn't prepared to do, it was throw up in front of someone as hot as Sir Pierce. It was embarrassing enough that he had not responded to her suggestive comments when she had assumed him to be a player in some kind of reenactment. If she could avoid making a further fool of herself in his presence, she would. Between his long dark hair, brooding brown eyes, and a beard that bordered lips she was sure would deliver a kiss she'd feel right down to her toes, he was the most handsome man she had ever seen.

She took several deep breaths, in and out, as he steered his horse off the track they'd been following. Soon they were sheltered by foliage and a congregation of tall oak trees that circled a small clearing. Once he had dismounted, he reached up to help her down from the horse.

'You're shaking,' he said, a frown weighing heavy across his brow. 'Are you cold? You must be.' He took off his cloak, which was made of thick black wool, and wrapped it around her shoulders with more care than anyone could have expected from a stranger. Besides a tear at one of the corners it was a fine garment, clearly of superior quality to any item of clothing Maddie had ever bought on Lincoln high street.

'Thank you, but I am not cold.'

His frown deepened. 'You think what those men called me back there is true, then. You need not fear. I am not a murderer, I am unjustly accused by a man who seeks to ruin my good name. I –'

Maddie held up a quivering hand. 'I do not think you are a murderer. Or at least, not one who wishes to harm me. Otherwise you would have left me to die back there. And, generally speaking, cold-blooded murderers aren't known for offering their cloaks to keep their intended victims warm.'

Sir Pierce blinked a couple of times. Clearly quite astonished. 'You believe in my innocence, though you do not know me?'

Maddie stared again into the brown eyes that had so entranced her when she first awoke. 'I believe you have shown me enough kindness to at least earn you the right to explain your side of the story.'

'But… if you are not succumbing to the chill and do not think me a murderer then… why are you trembling so?'

Maddie swallowed, hard. 'Before, when we were attacked, those were real arrows, weren't they?'

'Real arrows?'

'I mean they weren't… toys.'

Sir Pierce shot Maddie a look as though she were insane, and if what she thought had happened had *really* happened, she could understand why.

'No, lady,' the knight said. 'Lord Holtby and his men only fire arrows made to kill.'

'And… look, something very strange has happened to me. If this is some part of the convention, I didn't sign up for it and I… if you're in character, please break it now. I'm in dire need of help here.'

'Am I to understand that you think me some kind of player and this some kind of charade?' said Sir Pierce, rubbing his beard and shooting her a look of what seemed to be genuine puzzlement.

At this, Maddie couldn't help but chuckle. From his tone it was clear that the word 'player' didn't mean the same to him as it did to her. Still, she had to give him one last chance to break character. She waited for him to join in with her amusement and begin speaking in a more recognisable form of English. To assure her there must have been some mix-up at the convention and that he would take her back to the conference hall to find out what had gone wrong at once.

But he didn't.

And those arrows, they had come so close to hitting her. There's no way that would be permitted under health and safety law. And the overly formal way Sir Pierce spoke, and the men who called after them, right before they attacked. Their speech was recognisable as English but only just, to her ears. And then there was the fact that she had been transported somehow indoors to outdoors without her knowledge…

'How old are you?' she said, unable to ask the question she wanted to ask without raising Sir Pierce's suspicions even more than she obviously had done already.

'Why do you need to know that?'

'Just humour me with an answer, please?'

'I am thirty-three years of age.'

'Oh dear, I'm terrible with numbers so that would mean you were born in…' Maddie made a show of counting on her fingers and then adopted her most convincing perplexed expression.

'1515.'

She tried to temper her reaction but against her will she felt her eyes widen. She could see no hint of irony, no smirk of amusement on Sir Pierce's face. He was utterly earnest. By now, if he were a staff member at the convention, she felt sure he would have broken character.

'But it can't be…' she said.

'You think I look young for my years, my lady,' Sir Pierce said with a self-assured smile.

'No, that's… that's not what I meant…' She offered him a half-smile, trying to figure out what was going on. 'The last thing I remember was talking to Madame Codoni… and then she gave me a drink… Yes, that's it! The drink.'

One of two things had happened after Maddie accepted that cocktail from the fortune-teller. Either, she was magically transported back almost five hundred years in time or, more likely, she was so intoxicated by it that she had fallen, hit her head and was living out some kind of unconscious nightmare… or, with a chaperone like Sir Pierce, perhaps it was more a dream.

But everything felt so real…

'Codoni…' Sir Pierce repeated. 'Do you speak of that old crone that lives on the other side of the forest? The witch of Italian descent?'

Maddie frowned. If she was trapped in some kind of coma or strange trippy state after Madame Codoni's cocktail, perhaps there was some kind of subconscious escape route out of here. Maybe if Maddie visited this witch in her dream, who was somehow related to Madame Codoni, then she would be able to find a way to wake up. If it really had been the old woman's cocktail that caused her collapse, then that made some kind of convoluted sense. Just.

'There is a Codoni who lives near here? Can you take me to her?'

'At any other time I would oblige but –' Sir Pierce cut off sharply, raised a finger and tilted his head slightly to one side, as though he were listening for something.

'Wha–?' Maddie began but before she could finish her question, Sir Pierce had clamped a firm hand over her mouth and thrown them both down into the foliage.

With her mouth covered, she breathed heavily through her nose, taking in the scent of him: he smelled like woodland after rain and the feel of his hand over her mouth… well, it gave her ideas about what else those firm hands might be capable of. She was just beginning to enjoy that thought when the thud of horse hooves sounded. Not just one horse, but several.

'It's Holtby and his men,' Sir Pierce hissed into her ear. 'Do not make a sound.'

CHAPTER FOUR

ir Pierce held his breath as his foe trotted along the track several feet from them. He could just make out a few of the riders as they passed, peering into the forest on either side, but he had made sure they were well hidden by the surrounding foliage, and the procession passed too quickly to make a thorough inspection of the forest greenery. They had assumed, as Sir Pierce suspected they might, that he would follow the track out to the other side of Sherwood Forest in a bid to get as far away as possible. In essence, Holtby had assumed the same cowardice in Sir Pierce as he himself was capable of. And on that point, he intended to show Holtby that he was gravely mistaken.

Only when the thundering of horse hooves had completely faded away did he permit himself to breathe easily again, and release his grip on Lady Madelyn's mouth.

Gasping, she stared at him, her eyes so penetrating it seemed that she was staring straight through him. Between that, her odd questions and strange manner of speaking, he had no real idea what judgements to make on this woman. The fact that she had shown faith enough to believe him innocent however, prevented him from questioning her too rigorously.

'Why did you stop and allow them to catch-up with us?' she whispered. 'If we'd been discovered, that would have been the end of us both.'

Trying not to take offence in the lady's lack of trust in his ability to protect them, especially after he had saved her life but two hours ago, he answered: 'Less than a mile from here, just beyond a great oak tree that grows taller than any of the others, there is a small, abandoned cabin made of wood from this forest. I have used it as a place to rest my head on more than one occasion. Holtby's men will come across the cabin and search it. On finding nobody there they will resume their pursuit, believing we are still ahead of them. Darkness approaches. We shall take shelter in the cabin tonight and tomorrow it should be safe for us to go our separate ways.'

A look of alarm crossed her face. 'But I need you to take me to the Codoni residence. That is my only way of getting home. And I really, really need to get home.'

'You are lost? Tell me where it is you live, I may know it and be able to direct you.'

She let out a strange and bitter laugh that was just despairing enough to rouse some sympathy in him.

'I don't think that will be possible,' she said, her eyes lowering to the ground as though she felt some profound grief.

'Well, at least say the name so I might know for sure.'

'I... I can't tell you. It's... a complicated matter. You wouldn't understand.'

'I see, you think because I use my body to fight that I have no brains between my ears, is that it? I may not be a grand philosopher but I have had the education befitting my knighthood. Religion, poetry, chess, I know of all these matters, and more, in addition to my skills in battle.'

'Sir Pierce, no,' she said, shaking her head just rigorously enough that he believed her. 'Your plan to sleep in the cabin – a place Holtby's men have already looked – is cunning, as long as they don't decide to sleep there themselves of course.'

'They won't.'

'And even if you hadn't shared that plan with me, I wouldn't have doubted your intellect.'

'Then tell me, where are you from?'

She looked at him for a long moment and then sighed. 'Very well,' she said, pointing an accusing finger at him, but remember, you asked. You made me tell you.'

'I have only this second requested that you tell me, why would I need reminding?'

She gave him an almost piteous little smile. 'It's not a question of where I come from, but when.'

Sir Pierce looked at the lady side-long. Perhaps his first assessment of her being ill in the head was an accurate one. The woman had reverted to talking gibberish.

'Are you deliberately talking in riddles to prove your point about my intellect?'

'No, I'm trying to tell you something that is difficult to believe,' she said, pausing to take a deep breath. 'I'm not from another place… I'm from another time.'

Sir Pierce tried to allow this statement to make sense in his head without any further direction but it meant nothing to him. 'I'm not sure I follow.'

'I wouldn't expect you to, or anyone else to for that matter. I don't even know if this is a dream. If you are a dream. But I suppose if you are a dream, then no real harm can come of telling you that I'm from the future. The last thing I remember before I travelled here was talking to a woman called Madame Codoni. She must be an ancestor of the Codoni who lives here now. Or rather, the woman who lives here now must be an ancestor of Madame Codoni's. She's the only hope I've got of getting back to where I belong, and I have to get back.'

'I think, my lady, that you are not well,' he said, patting her creamy shoulder and allowing his hand to rest there a moment longer than was proper.

Lady Madelyn seemed distracted by his touch but a moment later her face was filled with pure incredulity. 'Oh, thanks a lot, mate.'

'Mate?'

'When you told me you weren't a murderer, I gave you the benefit of the doubt. But when I told you my truth, you didn't even take a moment to consider it.'

'That's because it's absurd.'

'I know that. But it doesn't make it any less true.'

Sir Pierce shook his head. This woman was a true mystery. One moment she seemed perfectly lucid, and the next ludicrous. She had even admitted that her tale of time travel was madness, and yet she spoke in earnest and expected him to give the story some credence. Her words about her believing his innocence stung him nonetheless. She was right on that point at least. She had no more reason to believe he was not a murderer than he had to believe she was from another time. But she had believed in him anyway. Though it was utter madness, he should at least give her the opportunity to prove her wild declarations.

'Do you have any proof?' Sir Pierce said, trying to keep the lack of conviction out of his tone.

'I... Yes!' Suddenly Lady Madelyn's face was brighter than the sun. Her smile broad and full, so much so that it made Sir Pierce want to smile himself.

Scrabbling up to her knees, she unhooked the small satchel she had been carrying across her person and handed it to him.

'Look in here. I bet you can't tell me what even one thing is in this bag.' There was a note of triumph in her voice that made Sir Pierce determined to identify at least one item no matter what.

Opening the satchel, he first placed his hand on... well, he couldn't quite say what. His confusion must have been written all over his face for Lady Madelyn giggled as he looked closer at the object.

'It appears to be a thin book of some nature, but it shines. And is rich with colour. I have not seen parchment like this before. Or people depicted in this manner C-os... Cosmo...'

'Cosmopolitan.'

'What does that mean?'

'It's... sort of difficult to explain in a way that will make sense to you. It's a magazine. I bought it for the train journey into Nottingham.'

'Train? It has something to do with the back of your gown?'

Lady Madelyn opened her mouth to speak but then closed her mouth again seemingly rethinking what she had to say. 'No... train means something a bit different in my time. Nevermind.'

'Oh. And what is the purpose of this... magazine?'

'Oh boy, that's a PhD thesis right there.'

'A what?'

'Nothing. It's for entertainment... merriment. A way to pass time.'

'Who is this lady, depicted here? How has the painter created such an intricate likeness? And why is she wearing so little clothing?'

Lady Madelyn covered her mouth with her hand to suppress yet more giggles. Though her amusement was at his expense, he found himself tickled by it. In addition to the most sumptuous lips he had ever seen it seemed she also had the most infectious smile.

'It's Mila Kunis.'

'What pray, is a Mila Kunis?'

'The woman in the photograph. In our time we have a... device called a camera. It captures images.'

'Very odd,' Sir Pierce said, eyeing the floppy book with great suspicion. 'Looks like witchcraft to me.'

'Oh yes, because of course, with all the powers of magic at my disposal I'd choose to use them to make a magazine featuring scantily clad women.'

Sir Pierce stared hard at Lady Madelyn. 'You do not speak in earnest, do you?'

'No! Ah, but there is something in here that will prove to you it is not witchcraft but technology.'

Lady Madelyn at once reached into the satchel and pulled out a small, flat oblong. She touched it merely for a second and the whole thing illuminated with a strange light, the likes of which Sir Pierce had never seen.

'No signal, out of area,' she said, her voice flat. 'I suppose that's to be expected.'

'You are expecting some kind of signal from somebody, my lady?' Sir Pierce enquired. He had no idea what kind of signal she could expect to receive from whatever magic box she held but the disappointment in her tone was unmissable. For reasons he did not quite understand, her clear displeasure left him wishing there was something he might do.

'Expecting is rather strong. Hoping would be closer,' she said with a small shrug. 'Here,' she leaned close to him. 'Let's take a selfie, and then you'll really be able to see what a photograph is.'

'A selfie, my lady? Sir Pierce said, and then started as he looked once again at the oblong in her hand. 'You have trapped us in that box! But how? What witchcraft is this?'

'Pierce,' she said, resting a hand on his arm in what was undoubtedly an overfamiliar manner which he should have taken exception to. 'You are still free and in the forest. You can still feel the air in your lungs. Feel the slight chill of the approaching dusk. I have trapped us nowhere. Just trust me, and watch what happens. I'm trying to show you something that nobody in this world has ever seen before.'

Sir Pierce nodded but kept one eyebrow raised as she instructed him to stare into the device. Once again she gave the magic box a mere touch and a moment later his image, the perfect likeness, flashed before him. He looked closer at the picture trying to understand how the camera, as she called it, had worked. He was no wiser for his looking but for some reason seeing himself sitting so close to Lady Madelyn made an unfamiliar warmth flood right through him.

'There, you see,' Lady Madelyn said, 'that wasn't painful, was it?'

'I suppose not... but how does it steal your image thus? Has it...' he tried to sound unmoved but the thought terrorised him. 'Stolen my soul?'

'Do you really believe I would do something like that?' Lady Madelyn said. And, gazing upon her again, he smiled and shook his head.

'Now, go on. Pick out something else.'

Reluctantly, Sir Pierce obliged. 'It's a rather odd leather pouch.'

'That's right. Why don't you open it?'

There was something about Lady Madelyn's tone that left Sir Pierce sensing some kind of trickery was afoot. And, sure enough, he was flummoxed. There were no obvious buttons or strings. Only a small piece of metal dangling from one side. As an experiment, Sir Pierce gave it a tug and a previously hidden hole began to open in the pouch.

'Keep going,' Lady Madelyn coaxed. 'It's called a zip.'

'Zip?'

Yet more hysterics from Lady Madelyn at him merely repeating the word. She drew closer, placing her hands over his as he opened the pouch wider. Her touch was surprisingly warm. Or was that just his reaction to her hands on his? Either way, there was no denying she was utterly distracting in every sense of the word.

'See,' she said, seemingly completely unaware of any effect she might be having on him. 'These cards? They are all ways of proving our identity in the future.'

Sir Pierce frowned. 'Why do you need to prove it? Why won't people take your word for it?'

'It's... a bit difficult to explain. But look, this one is called a driving licence.'

'You do not look pleased in this... phonograph.'

'That's very nearly right. It's called a photograph, and no. You're not allowed to smile on official documents like this one.'

'Why not?

'I… have no idea, actually. Here's my date of birth.'

'06. 02. 1989,' Sir Pierce recited slowly. 'These numbers do not mean anything.'

'Perhaps you record days of the year differently,' Lady Madelyn said, thinking quietly for a moment before speaking again. 'I was born on the sixth day of the second month. And you say we stand now in 1548. I was born in 1989. A little more than four hundred years from now.'

'Nay lady, it is not possible. There must be some error.' Sir Pierce said, swallowing hard. He had indeed never seen items such as these. There was something about them that was not quite of this world and though he did wonder about the lady's sanity, she certainly seemed sincere. Reaching into the bag once more, he pulled out a small silver square that rustled in his hands.

'What is this?'

'Ummm…' Lady Madelyn said, a slight blush in her cheeks. 'That's a condom.'

Sir Pierce stared at her. 'Now you are just making up silly words to have wicked amusement at my expense.'

'No, I'm not,' said Lady Madelyn. 'That is truly what it is called.'

'What does it do?'

'Well, when a man and a woman… consummate their feelings for each other, physically I mean, a man wears one of these to prevent disease, or a baby.'

Sir Pierce gave the woman a stern look. Having heard her explanation he was still convinced she was toying with him. 'How on earth would you wear something of this shape, and so small?'

'That's just a wrapping. If you opened it you'd find a… sort of sheath is the best way I can explain it, that fits over your… manhood.'

Sir Pierce looked inside the bag again, seeing an opportunity to play her at her own game of gentle ridicule. 'I count five of these my lady, how many men were you hoping to have encounters with today?'

Without hesitation she smiled. 'I was hoping to use them with just one partner, actually.'

It took a moment for Sir Pierce to digest what she truly meant by this and as he did, he felt his pole stiffen. If what he understood was correct, Lady Madelyn was a woman of great stamina.

'If you want a demonstration of how they work I'm happy to show you,' she added, her voice teasing and yet with a nuance to it that suggested she might well go through with her offer if he gave his consent.

Oh, what was this woman doing to him? She was so very bold. The kind of boldness that would make even a whore blush.

'But you said you already had a partner?' he said, feeling an odd, sharp stab in his chest as he acknowledged her prior words. 'You must be already wed to carry these and to be joining with another man with such regularity.'

The blush in Lady Madelyn's cheeks deepened. 'No, I am unmarried. Things work differently in my time, Pierce. People no longer have to be wed to go to bed with each other. In our customs, waiting until you are married to consummate your relationship is considered out-dated.'

Pierce was quiet for a moment as he digested this information. He was rather glad he had let her speak first for on hearing she was unmarried he was about to ask if she was a courtesan. He knew, from the redness of her cheeks that this would have been a dire mistake. This woman may be more brazen than any others he knew but she was not without modesty.

'Then I must seem almost backwards to you, my lady.'

Maddie smiled. 'Actually, I find old-fashioned chivalry deeply romantic. But I am sure my world sounds nothing less than barbaric to you.'

Sir Pierce considered her statement for a moment. The idea that women could offer themselves to any man they so wished, when they wished was a strange notion indeed. But then he had thought about the many women he had tried to woo who would not so much as kiss him for the sake of their chastity and reputation. Perhaps if that barrier were removed both he, and the ladies he had known, would have had a merrier time.

'I do not know what to think,' Sir Pierce said. 'But though your prior offer is more than tempting, I must make clear that my heart is already spoken for. As soon as I am found innocent of Holtby's baseless charges, I intend to propose to Lady Clarissa Bentley.'

'I see,' said Lady Madelyn, the disappointment more than apparent in her timbre. 'Then this is not a dream after all. If it were, I would already be in your arms.'

CHAPTER FIVE

usk was gathering when Maddie and Sir Pierce at last approached the cabin. As Sir Pierce had predicted there were no signs of life from inside. All was still. She had spent the brief ride between the clearing in the forest and here trying to overcome her humiliation at having been so forward with Sir Pierce. She reasoned however that she couldn't exactly be blamed. At first she had thought it was all a bit of fun. Part of a charade, and then she had thought this was a dream but as the coming chill of the night air pricked at her bared forearms, she was beginning to understand it was neither.

She still wasn't sure if Sir Pierce believed her story, and why should he, given that she could hardly believe it herself? Just now however, that didn't really matter. All that mattered was finding some way to convince him she needed escort to Codoni's ancestor. She recognised that being accused of murder was no small matter, and understandably he was focused on clearing his name. But if the present-day Codoni only lived on the other side of the forest, surely he could make a short detour? So far he had insisted he could not aid her but she had to find means of persuading him if she had any hope of seeing her mother again.

'By the look of your arms, you could use my cloak again,' he said, easing her down from the saddle.

She was about to stubbornly insist she was in no need of extra layers when the soft wool of his cloak enveloped her. She savoured the tender way in which he wrapped her up. She had spent so long caring for her mother, she couldn't remember the last time somebody had truly made a caring gesture towards her.

'What thoughts are running through that head of yours?' Sir Pierce said, his eyes twinkling in amusement. Before she met him, she had not known brown eyes were capable of such sparkle. His were nothing short of mesmerising.

'I – I was just wondering what we will do for light and warmth this evening,' she lied, scorning herself for letting her attraction to him show on her face. It must have done so for him to ask such a question and in truth, she had been wondering if they would need to sleep next to each other for body heat. That, in turn, had made her wonder how she would contain herself if they did.

'Fear not,' he replied with a knowing look. 'I always carry candles in my saddle bag. I will light a fire, it will be enough to stave off the cold and dark.'

'Carrying candles with you everywhere, that's impressive boy-scout behaviour.'

'Who is this Boy Scout of whom you speak? A suitor?'

Maddie laughed. She had done her best to speak in language she thought Sir Pierce had a chance of understanding but the odd phrase from her own time still slipped out. 'No… nevermind. It's not important. I was merely expressing admiration for how prepared you are.'

'A knight must always be prepared for anything,' he said.

Nodding, Maddie began walking towards the door of the small cabin. She stopped a few paces from the threshold, a thought striking her and her skin at once crawling. 'Will there be… spiders in there? Or… vermin?'

Now it was Sir Pierce's turn to laugh. And he did, heartily.

'What's this? The fearless traveller who leaps from century to century afraid of spiders.'

'I never said I was fearless,' Maddie said, feeling her eyes glazing with tears. She fought them back. Determined not to let what may not be anything more than a ridiculous dream get the better of her.

Something in her tone must have caught Sir Pierce's attention as when he spoke again his tone was much more gentle. 'You are afraid of something else? Not me… I venture?'

'No,' Maddie said, taking a deep breath. Maybe just admitting the fear would help her manage it. 'I fear not being able to return to my own world before it's too late.'

'Too late?'

'My mother is very sick. I have been caring for her for the last two years. The doctors are doing all they can but we don't yet know if she will live. And if I don't get back, she will think her only daughter has abandoned her. I can't let her face her illness alone.'

At that thought a single tear snaked down her cheek. Sir Pierce stood to face her and reached out a tentative hand to brush the tear away.

'Lady Madelyn, prithee do not cry. I cannot bear to see your tears. I will take you to the witch Codoni, but I need to find a way of proving my innocence first. If my whereabouts are discovered before that happens, I will likely be hunted down and killed before I can aid you.'

'Or propose to your dear Lady Clarissa,' said Maddie. Reminding herself again that Sir Pierce belonged to another – at least in his heart. 'I will find a way to help you prove your innocence.'

'How will you do that?' he said. 'Are you, involved with such matters in your… where you come from?'

'Not directly,' Maddie said, slowly. 'But I have binge-watched every episode of CSI.'

She smiled at the instant blend of confusion and frustration falling across Sir Pierce's face.

'I think I had better go inside and eradicate any unwanted creatures that might startle my lady,' he said.

'My hero,' she replied with a smile that was perhaps a little more flirtatious than it ought to be but she couldn't help herself. He had agreed to help, that was a huge step in the right direction. Her mother wouldn't die alone and she wouldn't die at the end of an errant arrow. Now all she had to do was figure out how to prove Sir Pierce wasn't a murderer. How difficult could that possibly be?

CHAPTER SIX

After Sir Pierce had cleared the cabin of several large spiders, caught them a rabbit for supper and cooked it over the fire, he and Lady Madelyn sat opposite each other on two upturned barrels. Between them stood the only piece of furniture in the entire cabin: a rickety old table.

'So, in order to clear your name, you need to tell me everything that happened,' she said. 'Including how you can be sure it was this Lord Holtby who committed the crime.' She sipped from his flask which he had filled with water from a source he knew to be pure, just a mile or so from where they now sat.

'I will tell you what I know,' he replied. 'Lord Edmund Holtby is enamoured with the same woman as I.'

'Lady Clarissa Bentley?'

'Correct,' Sir Pierce said, though something he couldn't quite put his finger on made him want to move on from this topic as swiftly as possible. Perhaps it was the comment Lady Madelyn had made earlier, about the fact that if this was a dream she would already be in his arms. He had found the comment rather touching and any man would no doubt feel privileged to have won the instant affections of a woman with Lady Madelyn's beauty. But, of course, he couldn't encourage her advances. Tempting though it may be. 'She is the daughter of Lord Richard Bentley and niece to Lord Thomas Bentley. Lord Thomas is the man who was murdered last night.'

'How was he murdered?'

'He was stabbed through the heart, with a sword.'

'Like the one you carry?'

'Yes, but I did not kill Lord Thomas.'

'Do you have an alibi?'

'A what?'

'Can anyone confirm where you were?'

'The killing took place late in the night, while Sir Thomas was sleeping. While everyone at the castle was sleeping – except the murderer.'

'So… you were alone? Lady Clarissa wasn't keeping you company?' Lady Madelyn raised her eyebrows in such a way that, even given their issues in communicating, it was impossible to miss her meaning.

'Goodness no! She is a lady. I wouldn't dream of touching her until we are wed.'

'I understand from our earlier conversation that you won't have consummated anything but are you actually trying to tell me you haven't even kissed this woman?'

'That is not how courtship works.'

'And you're going to ask her to marry you?'

'Yes.'

'But what if her kisses do not please you? What if she's bad at everything else too?'

'She's not.'

'Well, I can hardly take your word for it, from the sound of things you haven't even held eye contact with her.'

'If she needs schooling in the art of seduction then I will be only too happy to tutor her.'

This gave Lady Madelyn pause and her eyes worked up and down Sir Pierce's body in a manner that made him shuffle in his seat.

'What qualifies you to school her in that matter? Are you… experienced?'

'Enough to know how everything works.'

'How romantic,' Lady Madelyn said, her tone utterly flat.

Sir Pierce stared hard at the lady. 'You do not speak sincerely, do you?'

'Oh no, I'm sure she'll be weak in the knees for your working knowledge of human anatomy. Nothing to worry about there, at all.'

Sir Pierce cleared his throat. 'I fear we are rather getting off course.'

'Er, well, yes, perhaps you're right. So you were alone last night?'

'Ay, Lady. We were awoken this morning with the screaming and wailing of the castle staff, one of whom had found Sir Thomas dead in his chamber.'

'And why did suspicion fall on you?'

'Sir Holtby was at the scene before me and claimed to have found a strip from my cloak in Sir Thomas's room.'

'The tear at the corner...' Lady Madelyn said.

'Yes. The night before, however, my cloak had been in perfect condition.'

'So somebody tore your cloak and planted it at the crime scene... but how do you know it was Holtby?'

'He knew I was going to propose to Lady Clarissa this very night. And he knew that Sir Thomas approved of me as a match over him and would convince Sir Richard to accept me as his future son by marriage.'

'And Sir Holtby loves this... Lady Clarissa too?'

'I fear he is more interested in her father's riches than the lady herself.'

Lady Madelyn sighed. 'So, you have no alibi and there is, as far as anyone else is concerned, evidence that you were in Sir Thomas's bed chamber last night. We don't have any forensic evidence...'

'Forensic?'

Lady Madelyn waved a hand at him in a way that suggested she was trying to think. She did pluck odd words as if from nowhere in such a way that seemed to confirm her story about being from another time. The idea was, of course, absurd. But having found no other way to explain the objects he had found in her bag, he had to at least admit that she was from a faraway land. One that bore little resemblance to his own here in England.

'What we need is a confession,' said Lady Madelyn. 'We need Holtby to admit he was the one who ended Sir Thomas's life. If we can get him to admit that in front of Lord Richard, you will be exonerated.'

'There is no hope of Holtby confessing. The man has no conscience.'

'Well, we need to trick him into doing it.' Lady Madelyn fell silent for a moment. 'Lord Richard, is he a kind man?'

'Yes, I think him so.'

'Someone who might listen to a noble visitor from French shores?'

'What are you planning?' Sir Pierce asked, unable to keep the smile from his lips.

'Before, when I showed you the magazine. You said it was witchcraft. Everyone in this time believes witchcraft is real, don't they?'

'Many believe there are those that consort with the devil, yes, but why is that important?'

'I don't want to speak too soon,' Lady Madelyn said, her smile betraying a quiet confidence, 'but if you can get me to Lord Richard's castle tomorrow, then by sunset I believe his eyes will be opened as to who truly murdered his brother.'

CHAPTER SEVEN

addie awoke to a scuffling sound that made her blood run cold. She was blearily aware of some dim light from a candle, shining somewhere nearby. But she almost dare not turn around to get a better look at the cabin. The rustling sound was, she had decided, most likely a rat. Sir Pierce was sleeping close by, on the floorboards just as she was, but after a tiring day by anyone's standards, she decided that he would be less than thrilled to be woken to dispose of vermin.

Taking a deep breath, she slowly turned over towards the sound. Sir Pierce was sitting back at the table and turning the pages of her copy of Cosmopolitan by the light of his last candle.

Pressing her lips shut tight to stifle a giggle at the sight of a rugged knight taking such an interest in what was likely to be an article about leg waxing, she eased herself up off the floor and crept to his side.

'What are you doing?' she asked.

Sir Pierce jumped up in shock from the barrel he'd been sitting on and clutched the magazine to his chest. 'Nothing. I mean. I was just...'

Maddie reached out to pull the magazine away from him but he held onto it. 'Sir Pierce,' she said, with mock scorn. 'Why on earth won't you release my belongings?'

Sir Pierce pursed his lips and didn't respond.

'Well?'

'If I let go, you'll see what I was reading – or trying to read – and I do not wish that.'

'Why not?'

'Because a gentleman has his dignity.'

'Sir Pierce, whatever you were reading, I assure you, I will not think less of you for it. Come now, let go.'

Slowly, and with a surly frown, Sir Pierce did as instructed.

She turned the magazine to face herself and read the headline. '"Twelve Ways a Man Can Please You Better in the Bedroom." Why are you embarrassed to be reading this?'

'Because a man should just know how to please a woman. Unless a woman reaches the height of her pleasure no babes will be born. That aside, I would not wish to leave Lady Clarissa wanting. And after what you said before, it was clear you thought me lacking.'

A pang of shame hit Maddie for how hard she had teased him earlier about his sexual prowess. That was the kind of banter you could get away with in the 21st Century, but things were probably a little bit different here, five hundred years earlier. She tried hard not to dwell on the idea that she might well have hastened the spread of toxic masculinity centuries ahead of time.

'Sir Pierce, sit down, will you?' she said, her tone gentle. It was the first time she had used such a tone with him and he looked duly suspicious about what was coming next. Nevertheless, he took a seat and she pulled up a barrel next to him.

'The fact that you would try to read about how to better pleasure the woman you love – in a language that I'm sure is quite alien – is a wonderful, wonderful thing that few men, even in my time, would do.'

'So you... don't think me less of a man for it?'

'No,' she shook her head. 'You are much, much more of a man for it.'

The more she thought on this point, the truer it felt. Looking at him then, she could barely contain her lust for him. It was deeply unfair that he was already spoken for when he was this noble, this giving, this ruggedly handsome.

It was then a thought occurred to her. A wicked thought. But she had been so wholesome the past couple of years, hadn't she earned the right to be a little bit wicked?

By his own admission, Sir Pierce hadn't yet laid a hand on Lady Clarissa so they could hardly be considered together in real terms. Besides, she would, with a bit of luck, be home by tomorrow evening. This might be her only chance, in her whole life, to live a fairytale for real.

'The problem is,' she heard herself say while simultaneously deciding that she had earned her place in hell by saying it, 'that these magazines only offer a very general view of what a woman might enjoy in the bedroom. It's much better to gain real life experience. Tutoring from a real woman, that is, on how to create the maximum pleasure for a partner.'

Was it her imagination or was Sir Pierce's breathing deepening? Was he starting to realise what she was suggesting?

'Tutelage with no commitment...' he said, his voice soft, dreamy. 'For the purposes of education only, so I might better serve my lady when we are wed?'

'That's right,' Maddie said with a nod. 'It would need to be somebody wise in such matters, of course.'

'Such as a lady who expects one man to please her five times in one evening?'

Maddie smiled. 'Well, maybe not one evening. Maybe over a day or two... If you will have her.'

She tried to control her breathing but it was impossible to do anything but take deep gulps of air. If he denied her she would likely die of embarrassment, but she could not let this moment pass without at least letting him know that she would be willing to give her body to him, even if there was no hope of any lasting union. She was sure the memory would stay with her for the rest of her days.

'And you are certain this course will not in any way risk your reputation?' he said, his expression stern.

'No, my lord, we are safe when it comes to that.'

The frown that had lined his brow slackened. 'Then, lady, I would gladly have you,' he said, reaching out to her and running a hand through her hair.

'Pierce...' she whispered.

'Lady Madelyn, I await your instruction.'

CHAPTER EIGHT

e told himself this was in the service of better pleasing Lady Clarissa but in truth her blonde ringlets and icy blue eyes were far from his mind right now. How could anyone think of anything else, when a woman of such beauty and dignity offered herself?

When she had shed a tear for her ailing mother earlier that evening, shame had hit him like lightning. Shame that he had judged her as a wanton, and a mad wanton at that. When in truth, she had her own kind of integrity. A different kind of integrity than he was used to. More honest, more forthright perhaps. However one might describe it, there was no denying that it was most beguiling.

She had agreed there would be no commitments beyond their physical partnership. She seemed to have means of preventing the conception of a child. Why shouldn't he enjoy one last beautiful woman before he bound himself to his intended for life?

Following their agreement, the pair slowly rose from their make-shift seats. They surveyed each other in silence for a moment or two, though the air was thick with their want for each other. It was Lady Madelyn who moved first. Wasting no time in preparing herself for their joining, she pulled at the strings on her bodice. He watched with widening eyes as the sleeves of her green gown slipped from her shoulders revealing peachy, freckled skin now dappled in orange light cast by the nearby candle.

The garment hit the floorboards and he swallowed hard as he took in the alluring shape of her. She had removed her shoes before sleep and so stood barefoot and clad only in thin, black lace. Sir Pierce had never seen underclothes of this kind before. The drawers barely covered her most intimate areas. His eyes raked over her smooth, firm, legs which were also notably hairless. His breath faltered further as he fixed his eyes on the delicious curve of her stomach, and the strange contraption that elevated her breasts to the most awe-inspiring angles.

He could feel his jaw dropping as he looked at her, but he didn't care. It was only right that she understood just how the mere sight of her affected him.

She drew closer then, and began tracing her fingertips over the mail he had decided to sleep in. It was uncomfortable but he had slept in it many nights in times of battle and he had wanted to be prepared in case of ambush. That, however, was the furthest matter from his mind just now.

Though a thick layer of metal mesh still stood between his skin and hers, a searing heat burned somewhere deep inside at her slightest touch.

'I want to see your body, Pierce,' she breathed, her voice lower, huskier.

With some urgency he began to remove the mail which, once discarded, would leave him standing in nothing more than his breeches. She smiled knowingly as she assisted him in easing off the weighty armour. As though she somehow understood the effect this mere contact had on him and then slowly, oh so slowly, she pushed upwards on her toes. Just high enough for her lips to meet with his. And the moment that happened, Pierce could barely control his actions.

Grabbing her waist, he pulled her hard against his body, crushing his mouth against hers and swiftly finding her tongue. My God, she smelled so sweet. Like ripe fruit hanging from the vine, and the taste of her was like nothing he had ever known. It was as if she drank only the finest wines and the flavours lingered on her breath.

The warmth of her soft, naked body pressed against his was more than Pierce could stand and before he could stop himself, his hands squeezed and fondled her buttocks, which were barely covered by a whisper of lace. This seemed to please her, as she began to moan while circling his tongue with her own in a manner that made his rod pulse.

In the next moment he found himself lifting her onto the table, keeping his lips against hers as best he could whilst kicking off his breeches with more haste than he ever had before.

It was she who broke the kiss then. Pressing her hand against his chest in a bid to make him take a step backwards.

'Oh Pierce,' she breathed, running her eyes down his chest all the way down to his navel. Her eyes stopping, and widening, when they reached his pole. She bit her lip as she examined him. 'You are gorgeous.'

'You… mean that as a compliment?'

'Oh yes.'

'I have not heard that word used in such a way. But I am glad you approve of what you see.'

'More than words can express, so I suppose it makes sense that I find some other way to convey my admiration,' she said. Her smirk only made his shaft harder, though he wouldn't have thought it possible.

'The first lesson,' she said, at last dragging her eyes away from his body and meeting his stare. 'A true seduction takes time… and stamina.'

She passed her hands behind her back and unclasped the garment that had been holding her breasts in position. The view when she released her bosoms was enough to make him salivate. Two full and perfect rounds and two engorged nipples that begged to be sucked.

As though it were the most natural thing in the world to her, she lay flat upon the table. Her head at one end, her legs open wide at the other.

Reaching for his hand, she guided him to the end of the table where her head lay. She was smiling up at him. Her green eyes shimmering with what could only be read as excitement.

'Most men think that women are built like them and the first place they want stimulation is between their legs.'

'And that is... incorrect?'

Lady Madelyn shrugged and as she did so her breasts rippled in a manner that made it difficult to concentrate on her response. 'Sometimes it can work. But more often it's best to explore some other places first with your hands, your mouth and your tongue.'

'Nothing would give me greater pleasure,' he said bending over the table to deliver an upside-down kiss. She reached her hands up into his hair and he, unable to resist their allure any longer, traced his fingers down her chest and squeezed her breasts firmly in each hand. They were soft, warm, divine and as he tightened his grip her moans and whimpers increased in volume.

Slowly, he moved his mouth downward, along her chin and she turned her head exposing her neck. He licked every inch of it. Savouring the taste of her. The salt of sweat. The sweetness of her natural essence.

'Pierce, I want you... in my mouth,' he heard her whisper.

His muscles tightened at this idea. He drew back to meet her eyes once more. In them he saw only raw lust. The thought of her tongue lashing against his length almost brought him to his peak on the spot. 'But... what if I... can't contain myself?'

Her smile broadened. 'This is only our first lesson, I'm sure we'll have time for a follow-up before we part. And besides, it will give me the chance to school you in all the ways you can please a woman without penetrating her.'

The mere mention of penetration made his rod twitch. This didn't go unnoticed and without further delay Lady Madelyn hung her head a little further off the table, reached out for his pole and guided it inside her mouth. The instant sensation of her heat and warmth made his hips thrust without his bidding, pushing his pole deeper and deeper into her throat until he was buried to the hilt.

He took a moment to admire the body that lay before him. The temptress who held her lips so tight and firm around him. Reaching out for her breasts again, he toyed and groped and tugged at them while starting to gently drive his hips into her. Oh, the pleasure of it was overwhelming. The idea of this woman, this goddess, lying before him so willingly and offering herself for his pleasure in such a provocative manner – it was an experience he had not even dreamed of, unaware that such experiences were within the realm of possibility.

'Madelyn...' he groaned, squeezing her breasts tighter and tighter as he came closer and closer to his apex. 'I can't hold on, your mouth. Your body... they are too intoxicating.'

Without warning, Lady Madelyn reached her hands up to his buttocks and groped them with such force there was no hope of holding back any longer. Grinding his body into her face in desperation, he howled in heavenly fulfilment as his seed gushed and she swallowed every drop without a moment's hesitation.

CHAPTER NINE

'I want to lift you into my arms, but I can barely stand,' Pierce said, grazing her lips with a kiss before stroking her hair. He was still panting after all the pleasure she had brought him and a great warmth spread inside Maddie at that thought. Just knowing she could bring a man such as him to those heights made her feel more sexually powerful than she ever had before.

She sat up on the table which, so far, seemed just about to be holding her weight. 'That's alright. Just enjoy the moment. Take some time to rest.'

Despite his protests that he had no strength left in him, he still gathered her in his arms and pulled her down to the floor. Leaning his back against the cabin wall, he clinched her tight against his chest.

'I would be the one to pleasure you, as I understood it, not the other way around,' he said, before placing a kiss on the top of her head that was so tender it made her want to cry.

'Yes, that was the original plan,' she said, shaking off the strange teariness that had stirred the moment he'd wrapped his arms around her. 'But I got… distracted. You were standing there, so beautiful, I couldn't help myself. So in truth, you did pleasure me. Giving you pleasure, gave me pleasure.'

'Truthfully?' he said, drawing his head back a touch so he could look into her eyes and make some unspoken calculation about how honest she was being.

'Don't accept my word for it,' she said, taking his hand in hers and guiding it downwards, between her thighs.

She was still wearing her lace briefs but that wouldn't stop him from understanding just how much she had enjoyed having him in her mouth.

'My lady!' Sir Pierce said, the second his fingertips touched the sodden fabric.

'That's just what you do to me,' she whispered, leaning forward to steal another kiss from him. His lips were just as firm and forceful as she'd hoped and the way his tongue flicked over hers made her body writhe helplessly. His were the kind of kisses you spent your whole life dreaming about.

Mere moments later his hands pushed aside the lace of her underwear and his fingers teased her slit in such a way that she moaned hard into his mouth. Needing no more encouragement, he pushed his fingers deeper.

'Does that please you?' he asked, with the knowing tone of a man who already had his answer.

'Oh, yes, more than you can imagine.'

'What could make it more pleasurable?'

Maddie's breath caught in her throat as she realised this was the first time a man had ever asked her what she wanted, sexually speaking. Though her gasp was part-inspired by the surprise of being consulted, she was also somewhat shocked by the answer that began to form in her mind.

'I want...' she hesitated. What if her wants were not aligned with his?

Seemingly sensing her hesitation, he nudged her nose with his. 'Come now, we are rather past coyness... aren't we?'

'I suppose you could say that. Alright,' Maddie said, taking a deep breath. 'I want... I want you to put your free hand over my mouth and kiss my breasts while your fingers take me over the edge,' she said, trying not to cringe. She had no idea she could be so bashful. It seemed she was perfectly confident in the bedroom when it came to pleasing a partner, but it was only now she realised that she felt self-conscious about voicing her own needs.

'This is what pleases women?'

'No, this is what pleases me. Lesson number two,' she said, regaining some of her earlier poise. 'Women are individuals. If you ask a woman, as you have asked me, how to please them then you will find it difficult to fail them.'

A rakish smile spread across Sir Pierce's lips. He leaned close to her ear and murmured. 'I am only too happy to place my hand over that beautiful little mouth. I suspect if I don't her screams will wake every wolf in the forest.'

The only response she could muster was a whimper, full of longing and fuelled in part by disbelief that he could know just the words to heighten her excitement even further when she hadn't known them herself.

Seemingly satisfied with the reaction he had drawn from her, Sir Pierce pressed his lips against hers one last time before replacing his mouth with his hand. He then kissed his way down her neck. Her body arched towards him as he licked and nibbled his way to her breasts.

She watched him, as well as she could, suck hungrily on each of her nipples in turn as he worked his fingers in and out of her.

Why on earth did it feel so good to have his huge hand clamped so firmly over her mouth? She couldn't concentrate on analysing that right now, but he had been right about her screams. As he increased the speed and depth of his fingers, she was astonished to hear the sounds coming from her own mouth. They were somewhere between a squeal and a howl and the noise only seemed to spur him to work harder on bringing her to orgasm.

As he continued, she eagerly spread her legs wider to grant him better access.

'My goodness,' he said, breaking off his non-stop worship of her breasts. 'We are a wanton little whore, aren't we?'

The sound of those words, in his deep voice filled with raw lust, was too much for her to bear. There was no way on earth she would have let anyone speak to her that way in the past. But when Pierce said it, he coupled it with a grin that was almost boyish. It was part of the game. And there was nobody else she would rather be playing with.

At his words she felt her eyes begin to roll back in her head. He gripped her mouth tighter and his fingers pushed yet deeper and faster inside her. By this point her hips were thrusting violently into his hand. Craving the ecstasy only his touch could provide.

Lifting his head closer to hers, Pierce growled into her ear. 'I want to watch your face as you reach your peak.' He must have caught the pleading in her eyes, as he continued. 'I want to see the look of torrid fulfilment that only graces the faces of little whores like you.'

And that was it. Though part of her found the stimulation so divine she wanted to hang on, she simply couldn't. An orgasm that shook her entire body rattled through. Grabbing Pierce's arm, she dug her nails into his skin as she cried out in unanticipated ecstasy.

A moment later she was lying limp and shivering.

'You are beautiful…' Pierce said, removing his hand from her mouth and softly kissing her.

Slowly, she reached down for his other hand and dragged it upwards. Breaking off their kiss, she took his fingers into her mouth. She could taste her own arousal and the salt of his sweat as she held his eye.

'Lord help me,' Pierce said, shaking his head. 'You will make a philanderer out of me. Never in all my years have I met a woman like you.'

Sliding her lips off the tips of his fingers, she replied: 'And you never will again.'

CHAPTER TEN

rouching in the bushes at Sherwood Castle, Sir Pierce thanked the Lord it was at least a clement day. The castle gardens lay before him. He had walked the emerald labyrinth of those low, geometric hedges many times as a welcome visitor. An angry heat built inside as he thought about how, after all the years of training, focusing on little else but fencing and hunting in the service of his lord, he had been reduced to hiding in the bushes like a lowly criminal.

For the sake of making the time pass quicker while he awaited Lady Madelyn's return from her counsel with Sir Richard, he turned his thoughts to all that had passed the night before. Lady Madelyn may be gone from his life by tomorrow but she would be in his thoughts for the rest of his days. As promised, she had taught him much about the ways in which to best please a woman. Though he doubted very strongly that Lady Clarissa would have quite the same response to the words he had uttered to Lady Madelyn in the heat of the moment, and something about that thought left him deeply disappointed.

He had never spoken to a lady in that manner before and even now he could not fathom what had possessed him to utter such filthy slurs. Or what made them so delicious to dispense. Perhaps it was her request for him to cover her mouth with his hand. It had seemed odd to him when she first suggested it but his mind had quickly calculated how it might feel to imagine that she was at his mercy. Unable to cry out to man nor beast.

As had happened several times that day, his pole hardened in response to his remembrances of the night before. And it wasn't just the sexual encounter that had stirred him. With them both sated they had curled up in each other's arms, his cloak for a blanket, and lapsed into a long, luxurious slumber. It was the best night's sleep he could remember. He had felt utterly content, cradling her, relishing her softness and warmth.

Lord, the fire that woman brought out in him! It was both uncontainable and unignorable.

He had just begun to wonder if he had time to reach down and give himself a discreet stroking when his thoughts were interrupted by voices heading close to where he was hiding – a woman and a man. There was something familiar about them and it took him but a moment to realise that the woman was Lady Clarissa and the man was none other than Sir Edmund Holtby.

So, he had returned from his search for Sir Pierce. And now he was no doubt filling fair Clarissa's mind with all kinds of heinous lies about him and what he had done to her uncle.

'I don't know about this, Edmund,' Clarissa said as she brushed by, not five feet from where Sir Pierce was hiding. 'You were supposed to find Sir Pierce and put an end to him.'

On hearing this, Sir Pierce began to find it difficult to breathe. Why would Lady Clarissa say such a thing? And in that hard, cruel fashion. He had never heard her speak thus. Her voice was usually light and gentle. Clearly, she thought him a murderer without question. But how could she after the gentlemanly treatment he had shown her? Lady Madelyn had believed his innocence at once. Granted, he did save her from certain death but surely Lady Clarissa knew that he would protect her honour at any cost, even if there hadn't been an outright opportunity to do so.

'We searched the whole forest, my lady,' Holtby replied. 'It is my belief that he has fled for good. If he returns, all who know him are instructed to bring him back to this castle – dead or alive.'

'It is that last part that concerns me,' Lady Clarissa said, stopping in her tracks. 'If he returns alive, he might begin making accusations and put doubt in my father's mind as to who really killed Sir Thomas. And if my father uncovers the truth, I will not only be cut off from my father's riches but we will both likely be either imprisoned or executed.'

'He has no proof we played any part in your uncle's death, my lady,' Holtby said, his hands coiling around Lady Clarissa's narrow waist. 'Any accusations will just sound like the ramblings of a desperate man trying to escape retribution.'

'You had better be correct in your assumptions,' Lady Clarissa said, tapping away Holtby's hands. 'And don't get over familiar. You know you're not to touch me until we're married. I want assurances that my father's riches will come straight to us before you get any husbandly privileges.'

'As you wish my lady,' said Holtby, bowing just enough that his greasy mop of hair fell into his face. 'But let us make the announcement soon. I am sure news of our engagement will cheer your father at this difficult time. Especially without your uncle around to oppose.'

Those were the last words Sir Pierce heard from either of them before they moved too far away to glean anymore. As the true weight of what he had just overheard hit him, he fell to his knees and tried to breathe through the emptiness that threatened to engulf him. His fair Clarissa was part of the plot. All of her niceties, all of her charms as he had courted her over the last year, they had been nothing but a pretence. How long had she been plotting this? Weeks? Months? Ever since he had made his intentions to court her clear?

These and a thousand other questions swarmed in his mind as he realised he had been played for a fool. And now, due to his pitiful susceptibility to that woman's wiles, his very life hung in the balance.

CHAPTER ELEVEN

As one of Sir Richard's servants led her through breathtaking 16th Century interiors, it had taken every ounce of self-control for Maddie not to gape. The brief tour had culminated in being led into a reception room with a large open fire, dark wooden beams across the ceiling and two large chairs – almost throne-like, carved of oak and upholstered with thick, red cushions. She sat on one of these chairs now, awaiting Sir Richard's presence. She should be going over her story to make sure it was watertight and credible, but her surroundings were just too distracting.

She vaguely remembered doing a project on the Tudors at primary school but her nine year old brain hadn't found the intricate rugs woven in threads of turquoise and gold quite so marvellous. Nor had they found much interest in the delicate crockery or the intricate paintings hung in elaborate frames. But then, perhaps, seeing these items in their time, seeing how they were part of a person's existence, gave it all a different complexion.

'Madame Coustance, I believe?' came a deep voice from behind where Maddie was sitting. Coustance was the name Sir Pierce had told her to adopt. He had known a French family by that name long ago and, given how strange her way of talking was to the people of this time, they had agreed that it was best for her to pose as a visitor from foreign shores.

'Please my lord,' Maddie said, making a small curtsey to the man who fit the description Pierce had given her: a man with long greying hair, dressed in fine robes of richest blue. 'After the kindness your servants have shown me, I insist you address me as Lady Madelyn.'

Maddie took pains to speak at a considered pace, so far as she could without it seeming odd. She wanted to give Sir Richard the best chance of understanding her. With Sir Pierce's life in the balance, a barrier to communication with the man who might pardon him is the last thing they needed. It appeared to have worked as Sir Richard showed little hesitation when responding.

'Lady Madelyn, I understand you have asked for me personally?' Sir Richard said, surveying her with open curiosity.

'It is difficult to express my gratitude my lord, I am indebted to you for agreeing to this meeting at what I understand is a difficult time.'

'On the contrary, it is my pleasure to meet with a noble lady who has travelled so far. It is not every day that one receives a visitor from French shores. And, it is a welcome distraction from the loss of my brother. Please, sit.'

'It is the tragic loss of your brother that causes me to burden you with a visit, my lord,' Maddie said. She was fairly sure she was doing a good job of speaking in a manner appropriate for addressing a 16th Century lord. Largely, she was drawing on what she remembered about Shakespeare's writing from reading Macbeth at school. But she'd paid close attention to the way Sir Pierce talked since she had hatched her plan. Although, she admitted, that had little to do with executing the scheme and everything to do with the fact that she was mesmerised by him.

'What concern of yours is my brother's passing?' Sir Richard said, snapping her out of her thoughts.

'Firstly, my lord, let me say how truly grieved I was to hear of your brother's passing. My mother has been ill for a very long while.

I know what it means to face the loss of a family member you hold so dear.'

'Thank you, that is kind.'

'As to my prior point about your brother's untimely death, I was travelling north to visit family when my driver took a wrong turn and we found ourselves in the forest. Our coach was then beset by thieves. Only one of my footmen survived the attack.'

'How very frightful for you. You must be terribly shaken.'

'I was at first, my lord, but have largely recovered from the ordeal.'

'Forgive me, but I am uncertain how this turn of events is connected with my brother.'

Maddie took a deep breath. This was the moment where the plan could go one of two ways: either she would get a chance to convince Sir Richard of Sir Pierce's innocence or she would be incarcerated as a co-conspirator in his brother's murder. If there was one story she had to tell right, it was this one. 'I am only alive because of the bravery of one of the knights stationed at this castle, my lord. He could not save my other footmen from being slaughtered but he rescued me and one other from the savagery of those thieves. Soon after rescuing us, this knight went on to tell me the sorriest tale I have ever heard.'

'Was this knight who I think he was?' Sir Richard said, his tone at once much sterner. 'Are you speaking about the man who murdered my brother?'

'He identified himself as Sir Pierce, and said, as you do, that he was accused of murdering your brother. He did however go on to deny any wrongdoing, claiming he has been falsely accused. I was so grateful to him for his service and so moved by his tale that I felt compelled to come to you and suggest a partnership of sorts to ascertain the true culprit of this terrible crime against you and your family.'

For a moment, Sir Richard didn't speak and in that moment Maddie was sure that Pierce's worst case scenario, of her being locked in the castle dungeons, was going to come to pass. 'Do you know where Sir Pierce is now?' Sir Richard asked at last, his voice quiet, suspicious.

'No my lord. He escorted me as close to your premises as he dare, and then disappeared into the forest. But I am not easily drawn in. I know that wrongdoers often lie and deceive but the way in which he rescued me when he did not know me, when I could have been any stranger or even a threat to him, told me everything I need to know about his heart.'

'You do not believe he killed my brother?'

'No, my lord, I do not. He named another: Lord Edmund Holtby. Sir Pierce told me that Sir Edmund longed to marry your daughter but that your brother disapproved of such a match. And in order to ensure Sir Pierce would not be favourably chosen over him, Sir Edmund cut a portion of his cloak and left it in your brother's chamber after killing him.'

Sir Richard frowned. 'These are grave tales to be telling. Sir Edmund has been in service at this castle since he was a page. Sir Pierce on the other hand has only been in the service of this castle for several years.'

'I do not repeat this story lightly I assure you my Lord. However I felt compelled to relay this information to you because, if it were my brother, I should want to know who really killed him.'

'Even if what you say is true, Sir Edmund will deny it if asked.'

'Ay, my lord. But I think I have a way of finding out if he did play a part in your brother's demise. It will take a little cunning on our part. But if you are willing to keep an open mind until this afternoon, I believe you will know the truth about who killed your brother before sunset.'

Sir Richard shook his head in a way that made Maddie's heart sink but after a few moments reflection the lord raised his head to meet her gaze and asked: 'What must I do?'

CHAPTER TWELVE

Back at the cabin hideout, Sir Pierce dismounted and reached up to Storm's saddle to lift down Lady Madelyn. Their eyes did not meet. Though up until now he had taken great pleasure in looking upon her, after what he had overheard in the castle gardens he had, for some strange reason, not been able to truly face her.

'Pierce,' she said resting a gentle hand on his shoulder, seemingly sensing his anguish. 'Have I done something to displease you?

'No, lady.'

'I just thought you'd be more hopeful, given that Sir Richard has agreed to the plan, but you haven't said a word since we left the castle.'

Sir Pierce's chest tightened. Firstly at the thought that his silence could have caused this beautiful woman to think she had wronged him but secondly because he knew, for the plan to work, Lady Madelyn would need all the details. Which meant he had no choice but to speak of Lady Clarissa's betrayal.

He paused for a moment and then at last forced himself to look deep into those entrancing green eyes. 'Holtby' he said, 'was not acting alone when he arranged for me to be falsely accused of murder.'

'He had an accomplice? Who?'

Again Sir Pierce hesitated but he forced the words passed his teeth. 'Lady Clarissa.'

Lady Madelyn's eyes widened. 'Pierce, are you sure?'

He offered her a slow but definite nod. 'I heard them talking in the gardens while I hid. They plotted it. They plan to marry.'

She shook her head in what seemed to be part disbelief and part sorrow. Then, without a word, she wrapped her arms around his neck and pressed his head softly against her shoulder. He breathed in her tantalisingly fruity scent as she enveloped him. And in turn he looped his arms around her waist, pulling her close. The sensation of her soft body, nestled into his, made the pain feel farther away.

'I am so very sorry,' she said with a genuine ache in her voice.

For as long as he could remember his life had been devoted to hard battle and brutal training for whenever the next battle might arise. His exchanges with Clarissa had always been cordial, as was proper, but he was unable to call to mind the last time anybody had held him like this. Perhaps when he was a boy of five or six, just before his mother died. Though his father outlived his mother by three years he was not known for his affectionate behaviour. Lady Madelyn's open offering of tenderness was a gift for which he thanked the heavens. How he would have braved this blow alone, without her, he did not know.

'I do not deserve your kindness,' he said, tears swelling in his eyes at the confession. 'I was a fool to be so blinded.'

'Hey,' she said, withdrawing from their embrace so she could look at him once more. 'All you did was trust. It is she who is at fault. Don't let someone like that blacken your heart. Or make you believe their betrayal has anything to do with you. In truth it says everything about her. Personally, I think she's mad. I caught a glimpse of Holtby when he was firing arrows at me. He is greasy-haired and flat-nosed and doesn't hold a candle to you. You are the most beautiful man I have ever met Sir Pierce, inside and out. The loss is hers.'

Instinctively, Sir Pierce pulled her body back into his and kissed her. It was a liberty, perhaps, but she did not resist. He at once remembered how right it felt to press his lips against hers. His tongue searched for her tongue. His hands gripped her closer, before roaming downwards to grope at her delectably round buttocks.

This gesture caused her to moan. He had learned last night that her moans were the sweetest music, and each time she made such an utterance it only spurred him to tighten his grip on this strange but enchanting woman.

When their lips parted, they both panted and tugged desperately at each other's clothing.

Lady Madelyn sighed and reluctantly pulled away. 'I fear we will not have time for another... lesson before Holtby is upon us. We cannot leave anything to chance. I believe Sir Richard will send him to the agreed meeting point but you must go and hide yourself. If Holtby senses the trap, I will never be able to clear your name.'

'You...?' He paused.

'What?'

'You do still want to... tutor me then?'

Lady Madelyn raised a sultry eyebrow. 'Why would I not?'

'The agreement was that you were tutoring me to better seduce Lady Clarissa. And now of course, no such thing will happen.'

'Don't you know what a cunning witch I am by now, Sir Pierce?' she said, her voice full of good humour. 'That was just an excuse to get my hands on you.'

After the cruel betrayal he had so recently suffered he didn't expect to laugh anytime soon. But laugh he did, and he kissed her again. 'I will do as you bid me if you promise me one thing.'

'And what might that be?'

'If this plan succeeds, if I am proven innocent and we live, then tonight we will join in the luxury of Sir Richard's Castle. Grant me one more night at your side before I must return you to whatever strange land you appeared from.'

Lady Madelyn stroked his long, dark hair and then held his face in both of her hands. 'How could I ever resist you?'

CHAPTER THIRTEEN

addie had agreed with Sir Richard that he would dispatch Holtby to the cabin, claiming he had heard that this was where Sir Pierce was, at present, hiding out. To ensure Holtby did not connect her with Sir Pierce however, Maddie had instructed her handsome knight to ride her a good mile from the cabin, to a spot on the forest track Holtby would undoubtedly take.

Tethering Storm somewhere in the depths of Sherwood Forest, he then hid himself amongst the thick foliage while she began to yet again to go over the plan in her mind.

By the time Maddie heard horse hooves thudding along the track, she had fashioned Sir Pierce's cloak into a shawl and hood using the removable leather straps from her satchel. Her heart thundered at the thought of all that was at stake. But then, the vision of having Sir Pierce all to herself in a chamber at Sir Richard's castle was more than enough motivation to give her deception of Sir Edmund Holtby everything she had.

The moment Holtby caught sight of Maddie, he slowed his horse to a trot and when the beast was level with her, he brought his steed to a standstill. Though his helmet obscured most of his face, Maddie could see from his rigid posture and the manner in which he looked down at her from his saddle, that he thought himself extremely important.

'Tell me, peasant, have you seen a Knight of King Edward ride this way?'

'Nay, my lord,' Maddie replied in the quiet, alluring voice she had been practicing during her wait. 'But I can say, you will be successful in finding he whom you seek.'

A sneer spread across Holtby's lips. 'And pray, how might you know such things?'

'I am a seer, my lord. It is a gift I've had since birth. And the moment your horse came galloping into sight I had a sense of a future far greater than most could imagine.'

'Is that so?' Holtby said, dismounting his horse and removing his helmet. 'I don't put much stock in such tall tales.'

Maddie smiled. She had anticipated Holtby's scepticism and during her conversation with Sir Richard had procured some information that would make a believer out of him.

'If I do not speak true, my lord, how would I know that your mother used to wear an emerald necklace given to her by her own mother, and passed on to you for your future bride?'

This gave Holtby pause but then he shrugged. 'Perhaps you knew my mother.'

'Nay my lord, as you can tell from my voice I do not hail from these parts. I am from France and have only come to Sherwood in recent times. Yet, I know about the first time you ever shot an arrow. You accidentally shot your own foot.'

'How do you know this? Are you some kind of spy?'

'No my lord, in truth it is as much a mystery to me as it is to you how I see these visions. All I can tell you is that I see them. Whenever I meet a person I can tell them truths about their past and truths about their future.'

Holtby looked at her side-long, weighing up her explanation. 'Very well. I will humour you. You mentioned some manner of great future for me. Of what greatness do you speak?'

A mysterious smile curled Maddie's lips not dissimilar to the ones Madame Codoni had flashed at her. This was the big moment. She could only hope Sir Richard had, as they had agreed, manoeuvred himself into a position close enough to hear what would follow if all went to plan. Waving her hands in the air as though touching some invisible current, she spoke to him. 'I see you rising the ranks of nobility,' she said, unable to remember the exact wording from Macbeth but remembering that the witches had convinced a soldier he would be king. 'The throne of England itself is within your reach.'

'The throne? Surely ye cannot speak true?'

'I can only tell you what I see my lord, but be assured that in all the truths I have seen, I have never been wrong… But wait, oh no!'

Maddie withdrew a couple of steps and looked upon Holtby with wide, fearful eyes.

'What is it?' Holtby asked with a frown.

'The picture of your future is changing this very instant. This has never before happened. But something has changed your future, yes! The throne of England could have been yours, but now no more because of a grand deception. You have tainted your future, my lord. Your plot with Lady Clarissa to kill Lord Thomas and make the world think it is somebody else's doing, this truth has sullied the future that could have been yours. You will be found out. The world will know what you have done. And now no man will be willing to call you their king.'

At first a look of quiet astonishment played out on Holtby's face. But a moment later he gritted his teeth and snapped at Maddie. 'I don't know how you came by these truths, witch. But you will never get a chance to tell anyone what you know. I will have my throne. My secret sin will die with you.'

Holtby drew his sword, grabbed Maddie's cloak and threw her into the moist soil.

'That was not a prudent course for you, wench. Consorting with the devil to learn truths not for your eyes or ears. And now the punishment will be death!'

Holtby raised the sword above his head. Maddie gasped, watching the dim light of the forest glint off the blade as Holtby brought down his weapon with vicious and unstoppable force.

CHAPTER FOURTEEN

oltby's blade was less than an inch from Lady Madelyn's nose when Sir Pierce intercepted it with his own sword. The clang of the blades clashing together sent Lady Madelyn reeling backwards in shock. She stared up at Sir Pierce, startled but visibly relieved that he had reached her in time.

'Sir Pierce!' Holtby spat. 'I should have guessed it. So, you are in league with this witch? You should know that no dark power on this earth can help you now. Sir Richard thinks you guilty and has instructed me to make sure you are disposed of once and for all.'

With this, Holtby swung his sword at Sir Pierce, who niftily dodged the blade.

'To think I once fought alongside you as a brother-in-arms,' Sir Pierce hissed through gritted teeth. 'It sickens me that you have become no better than a mercenary. Why would you abandon your knightly duties like this? Sir Richard has given you a home and purpose since you were but a page. How could you kill his brother?'

'Sir Richard is an amiable fool who has no idea how to use the riches and powers bestowed on him,' Holtby snarled. 'His brother, Sir Thomas, disapproved of me only because I had vision. Together, Clarissa and I will be the most powerful nobles in England.'

'And power is worth all you have done? Murder? Betrayal? Conspiracy?' Sir Pierce countered, knowing that Sir Richard must be taking cover somewhere close and thus must have heard Holtby's confession.

'If you are fool enough to ask that question, then you deserve to die,' Holby snarled.

Without further hesitation, Holtby swiped his sword left and right, up and down as he advanced on Sir Pierce. At every turn, he blocked Holtby's stabs and thrusts, whilst retaliating with a few of his own. Sir Pierce's blows became increasingly vigorous as he remembered how Holtby and Lady Clarissa had toyed with him over the last year. Manipulating him into believing Lady Clarissa would consider him as a suitor, when all along he was to be a scapegoat for their plot. Their vindictiveness had almost cost him his life, and moreover had caused him to shun and discourage the affections of a lady who was deserving of his attentions: Lady Madelyn.

Sir Pierce felt as if his very blood was on fire as he once again recalled the look of disappointment on his lady's face when he told her his heart belonged to another. And the agreement they had made to enjoy each other physically without any commitment. She deserved better than such callous treatment after the way she had stood by him and aided him in proving his innocence. He had acted so out of a sense of obligation to a woman who had plotted his demise. None of this however, compared to the rage that had filled him when he watched Holtby raise his sword in a bid to end Lady Madelyn's life. And as he fought his foe now, this thought is what spurred him to strike at his opponent's sword, again and again with such unceasing force that in mere moments Holtby was driven to his knees, his sword fallen to the ground.

Sir Pierce held his blade against Holtby's throat and tilted his chin upwards. 'Give me one reason why I should let you live,' Sir Pierce growled.

'Because his fate should rest in my hands, Sir Pierce,' came Sir Richard's call as he emerged from the foliage with several other knights in tow. 'As he murdered my brother, I believe I have the right to deal with him in my own way.'

Slowly, Sir Pierce withdrew his sword and turned towards Sir Richard, offering him a small bow. 'I will abide by your will, my lord.'

'Fortunate that you should be riding by when Lady Madelyn was in need of your help,' said Sir Richard, casting a knowing look at Sir Pierce. 'When I spoke to the lady earlier she did not know where you had ridden to.'

'Ay my lord,' Sir Pierce replied. 'Twas fortunate I came riding by.' Though Sir Pierce was in no doubt that Sir Richard knew they had lied to them on this point, he was not about to freely admit to it. With several other knights in attendance, his lord would have no choice but to make an example of him if he openly admitted deceit. Given the lie was a small one, and it was told in the interests of keeping himself alive, it seemed best to let Sir Richard focus on the bigger matters at hand. And on that score, his lord wasted no time.

'Is it true what you say of my daughter, and her part in this?' Sir Richard asked, turning to Lady Madelyn, who was now standing at the edge of the forest track, Sir Pierce's cloak wrapped around her shoulders. Her face still quite pale after Holtby's assault.

'I believe so, my lord,' she said. 'Sir Pierce overheard a conversation between your daughter and Sir Edmund in the castle gardens. Exactly what part she played in your brother's death, I cannot say. I am sorry you found out as you did. I did not learn of your daughter's involvement until after our meeting earlier today.'

Sir Richard offered a sorrowful nod and then turned on Holtby. 'I will know all there is to know about my brother's untimely passing. And as for your betrayal, it is a crime that cannot be undone. To turn on the very house that has sheltered you and fed you for years is unspeakably despicable. I do not hold high hopes of you seeing another winter.'

'It was your daughter, my lord,' Holtby tried. 'She tricked me. I would never –'

Sir Richard held up his hand. 'I will hear no more until we return to the castle where Lady Madelyn will be our honoured guest, if she so chooses, to shelter with us for the night.'

Lady Madelyn shot Sir Pierce a knowing glance that at once sent a searing heat through him before she replied. 'Ay my lord, it would be my pleasure.'

And secretly, Sir Pierce vowed that the pleasure would indeed be hers.

CHAPTER FIFTEEN

The last few hours had been pure torture. The irony of such a sentiment was not lost on Maddie, given there was likely to be a literal medieval torture chamber in the dungeon of the castle, where she believed Sir Edmund Holtby was at this very moment paying dearly for his betrayal. Having so recently lost his brother, Sir Richard was in too much grief to decide on what penalty his daughter would pay for her part in her uncle's murder. According to the snippets Maddie overheard from gossiping servants however, they suspected Lady Clarissa would be sent away from the castle and cut off from all riches she would have otherwise inherited.

Surrounded by so much sorrow and drama, Maddie knew it was wrong to be focused on selfish concerns, but after putting the needs of others before her own for so long she had managed to convince herself it was acceptable, just this once, to concentrate on the barrier to her own gratification. Namely, that the people at Sir Richard's castle had spent the evening finding new and ingenious ways of keeping her from Sir Pierce's arms, which had proven to be her own personal brand of medieval torment.

First, Sir Richard was adamant that she be given a full tour of the castle. Then it was insisted upon that she attend an evening meal of five courses. Some of the offerings she had politely forked into her mouth, she had not even recognised and in one or two cases it had taken real effort not to show just how disgusting she found the texture of the dish. Still, the goose meat was tender, and the tart for dessert was sweet.

She was sure that, once the formality of dinner was finally over, Sir Pierce would find a way of excusing them from the proceedings. Instead he hissed into her ear, just as the servants were clearing away the dishes, that he would have to sneak into her room after everyone else was asleep as going there directly would cause outrage considering they were not wed.

Pleading tiredness, and holding aloft a candle, she had then made her way to her bedchamber. Sensing that she might have a long wait for Sir Pierce, she had also asked one of the servants if she might have some hot water to bathe in. A short while later, pans of boiling water were provided and poured into a wooden bathing tub that looked more like a barrel than anything else. The servant took great pains to emphasise that the soap was scented with lavender and, guessing this was deemed a luxury, Maddie made a show of sniffing and appreciating the smell.

After all she had endured in the last twenty-four hours, a bath was long overdue and once she had finished cleansing herself, she also washed the worst of the mud stains out of her dress and gave her underwear a scrub before laying it all on a chair near the fire to dry.

Having nothing else to wear, she was completely nude as she climbed into the lavish bed, over which hung a decadent red canopy. She smiled at the thought of Sir Pierce's arrival, and all that would follow.

She was almost asleep when she at last heard the lightest of knocks and her chamber door was eased open.

Sir Pierce smiled, checking it was agreeable for him to enter. By candlelight, Madelyn beckoned him in. The moment he had her invitation he whipped inside and closed the heavy door.

'You look different,' she whispered as he hurried towards the bed.

'Yes, well I finally had a chance to take my mail off and find something more comfortable to wear, though perhaps less dashing.'

'Oh, I see. We think ourselves dashing, do we?' Maddie teased as she eyed the white linen shirt and black breeches Sir Pierce had changed into. This was the tender, vulnerable man behind the shield and beneath the mail. In the short time she had known him, she had seen both his physical grit and his sweetest tenderness. The combination of the two left her weak.

There was a slight blush in his cheeks after her prior comment. 'You are correct, my lady. It is not for me to say whether I am dashing. I do not wish to appear arrogant.'

Maddie chuckled. 'Actually I think you are deeply modest. If I looked like you and fought like you I'd probably be the most arrogant man alive.'

Sir Pierce joined in her gentle laughter. As he made his way over to the bed, he glanced over at the fireplace and at once flashed her a devilish grin.

'You look like a man with terrible intentions,' she said, smiling back at him.

'I couldn't help but notice that all your garments hang by the fire, my lady.'

'They do.'

'And you have no other clothes.'

'I do not.'

Without another word, Sir Pierce grabbed the thick red blanket Maddie had been hiding under and tore it away. She squealed as he did so, not expecting him to be so forward after his cordial behaviour during this interminable evening. Perhaps the wait over dinner had been as long for him as it had been for her.

His eyes dropped from hers and gorged on her body. 'Oh my lady, I hope you took the time to rest while waiting for me for I shall not let you sleep a wink tonight.'

Pierce tore off his shirt and in a flash his muscled torso was locked between her thighs. The weight of him on top of her was strangely comforting, perhaps because she had been inexplicably dragged across the centuries by some meddling crone. Pierce's body felt like an anchor to this time and place, and there was something steadying about that.

Softly he stroked her auburn hair and looked deep into her eyes. He leaned in to kiss her but then hesitated.

'Is something wrong?' she asked, for a moment crushed by the idea that he might be having second thoughts about spending the night together.

'I fear I have not made something clear.' He looked almost pained as he spoke and, on seeing his expression, Maddie suddenly found it difficult to breathe.

'Go on,' she prompted. As attractive as she found Sir Pierce, she was not interested in going any further if he was acting out of some sense of duty to her for helping him prove his innocence.

'I have the deepest respect for you, Lady Madelyn. Though I spoke to you in a callous manner when we engaged in our last... lesson. I want you to know that I hold you in high esteem and hope my open display of lust for you has not given you the impression that I think you lesser.'

Maddie waited a moment before speaking again. 'Is... that everything you wanted to say?'

'Ay, my lady. I just needed you to know.'

Relief crashed through her and she smiled. 'Do you think I would lie with a man who I believed didn't hold me in high esteem, as you put it?'

Pierce paused for a moment and then laughed. 'No,' he said, 'I do not believe you would.'

'Then let us not delay our pleasure any longer,' she said, tracing her nails down his back. 'I will not be here forever, we must make the most of the time we have.'

A coldness came over her as she said those words and she realised, with some surprise, that the connection she felt to Sir Pierce wasn't just physical. Perhaps it was the fact that he had saved her life not once but twice in the brief time she had known him. Or perhaps it was watching him suffer the betrayal from Lady Clarissa. Seeing him so terribly broken by a woman who didn't deserve a man like him had made her realise just how many fine qualities he had.

Or perhaps it was the thing she had been trying to ignore most of all. That some part of her heart had recognised him the second his eyes had first looked into hers. Whatever the reason, she needed to make sure she managed her feelings carefully between now and dawn. There was no point getting attached to him when tomorrow, in all likelihood, she would be leaving his side for good.

'A knight, who never knows which battle will be his last, excels at living for the now... carpe diem,' he said, jerking her out of her thoughts. 'I will not disappoint you.'

And with that he was kissing her. His firm lips pressed hard against her own and she opened her mouth to him so that the kiss could deepen. She could barely contain her need as his tongue flicked against her own, and her hands grazed their way down his navel until they reached his hardened cock, which she stroked through the fabric of his breeches.

Her teasing massage had its intended effect as he began tugging off the garment, the only barrier now between them. The second he was free of them, her legs clamped back around his body of their own accord. The moisture between her thighs telling him, without any need for words, just how much she wanted him.

CHAPTER SIXTEEN

'Oh, my lady!' Sir Pierce growled. 'You are so very... so very...'

'Wet,' she finished for him. 'I am so very wet. For you.'

The boldness of her words only made his pole strain harder against the irresistible silkiness of her most private nook.

'I must taste you as you have tasted me,' he said, 'What I mean to say is, I wish to do so... if that would please you?'

'Oh,' she sighed, stroking a hand over his beard. 'Yes, I imagine it would.'

Slowly, he began kissing his way down her neck, pausing to pay extra attention to her breasts, which seemed particularly sensitive. Each time he circled his tongue around her nipples or squeezed at the cushioned softness of them, she let out a little whimper of delight and her body arched towards him.

'Lesson number three,' she gasped. 'Though I'm not sure you need it, stimulating your lover in more than one manner at a time is likely to yield very, very positive results.'

Smiling, he kept his grip on her breasts as his mouth continued its journey southwards. Whilst squeezing those delightful orbs, he lashed his tongue over her flesh, relishing the sweet taste of salt and the fragrant scent of lavender that seemed to emanate from her every pore. As soon as he approached the point where her thighs met he began delicately kissing the soft down he found there. Taking his time to cover her in kisses before noticing that for every inch lower he kissed, the stronger his lady's reaction.

Never had he experienced this kind of intimacy with a woman and never had he held this kind of power over one as he began to lap at her sweet, sweet nectar. The first delving of his tongue made her whole body convulse. Sir Pierce smiled up at the sight of her breasts covered by his big hands and beyond, her mouth open, and gasping. By the time he had made her his once and for all, he intended to leave her even more breathless than she was now.

Lowering his head again, he gently teased her opening before gradually driving deeper and deeper. With every lick her body rippled in response and yet more nectar flowed. As her body thrashed and writhed at the bidding of his tongue, he mimicked the rhythm he would like to create when he finally entered her with his pole, which was throbbing harder for such fulfilment with the lady's every unearthly moan.

'Pierce,' she almost wailed, as though reading his very thoughts. 'I need you inside me. I need you inside, please!'

Reluctant to change his position so soon and yet unable to resist such a desperate appeal, Pierce kissed her once more on each thigh and then pushed up onto his knees.

She was already fumbling with a condom, as she had called it, pulled from her bag on the bedside table. He watched with a blend of interest and curiosity as she tore open the odd square he had first looked upon just a couple of days ago. What she produced from the square was even stranger, almost alarming in fact.

With a ravenous flicker in her eyes, Lady Madelyn crawled towards him on the bed and wrapped her mouth around the tip of his pole, swirling her tongue around and around in a manner that almost left him dizzy.

'My lady,' he hissed, 'if you wish our joining to last any time at all I implore you to halt at once.'

He heard a muffled little giggle before she took his manhood in her hand and rolled the strange contraption along the length of him. He saw now, how it worked. It was not so dissimilar to the linen sheaths that some were said to use in such intimate situations.

Seemingly satisfied that all was in place, Lady Madelyn lay back on the bed, beckoning him with her finger.

He needed no other prompting to draw closer and position his rod at her entrance, slowly, gently sliding inside as he stretched out on top of her body. Gradually, but deliberately thrusting his hips to achieve the maximum depth.

'You feel…' he began but she was so tight and warm and slick he could not finish the sentence. 'Mere words cannot capture how you feel.'

'You're so deep… so very deep,' she murmured before he covered her mouth with a kiss. Gently, he began drawing back and driving into her in a steady rhythm. Remembering how she had responded when he had spoken to her in a playfully undignified manner the night before, he decided to try his luck with that tactic once again. But this time, perhaps, he would take matters further.

'You seem to be enjoying my manhood, my lady,' he said, making sure that she caught the tenderness in his eyes as she looked at him.

A funny little smile graced her lips as she replied. 'Yes, you're taking me so hard. So fast…'

'My sweet little whore, I haven't even started,' he said, increasing his depth and speed just a touch to prove it.

'Oh, Pierce,' she cried, her breasts rocking back and forth with the force of his love-making, her eyes rolling backwards at his words, her hips rising to meet his own.

Pleased with the effect he'd had on her, he took his talk a step further. 'I think a good little whore like you can take it a lot harder and deeper than this. And I plan to put it to the test. We will soon both reach our peak, that much is certain. But shortly after, I will take you again and again until I am satisfied. Do you understand?'

'Yesss,' his lady hissed out.

He noticed a slight shake in her limbs which last time had been the beginning of her explosive climax. At that thought, he felt his own apex approach, but he had to hold on. He wanted his lady satisfied, and nothing was going to compare to the sheer wonder of feeling her body shudder around him as he pushed her over the edge.

Gripping her breast in one hand and her throat in the other, he kissed and nibbled at her lips while driving into her at an uncontrollable pace. 'I want to see you tremble,' he groaned. 'I want to see my little whore in ruins.'

These words, it seemed, were the last provocation she could take as at once she shoved her body wildly against his and cried out at such volume that he at once clamped his hand over her mouth for fear one of the servants would hear and think the worst of him. This gesture only seemed to spur her to greater heights and the tight, rhythmic spasms of her body around his pole pulled him over the edge with her. So intense was his own peak he had to bite his lip in a bid to keep his moans low enough that only she could hear.

'My lady,' he gasped breathlessly as that glorious rush crashed through them both, 'my sweet, sweet lady.'

'My lord,' her delicious, husky voice replied.

CHAPTER SEVENTEEN

A rosy dawn shining through the red curtains caused Maddie to stir the next morning. Gradually, her eyes prised open, only to meet those of Sir Pierce. He had, it seemed, been awake for some time and been watching her sleep.

'Hi,' she said.

His first response was to encircle her in his strong arms. As he did so, she breathed in his intoxicating scent. Even now, he smelled of the forest.

'My lady,' he replied.

'How long have you been awake?'

'I only slept a short while.'

'Is something wrong?'

'Quite the contrary, I was too full of joy to close my eyes. Knowing that I must say goodbye to you today, I wanted to commit this beautiful face to memory.'

Clasping his face in both of her hands, she raised herself to administer a slow, gentle kiss.

'You talk in your sleep,' he said, when their lips parted.

'Oh no,' Maddie said. 'It has been known but, it's been a while since anyone's been in a position to tell me about it. What was I saying?'

'Something about a… a hamster… what's a hamster?'

'It's an animal, a pet you might keep as a child,' said Maddie. 'Ever since my mother became ill I've been having dreams about my old pet hamster dying.'

Sir Pierce tightened his embrace. 'I wish I could shield you from that pain.'

'Knowing that you want to do that for me makes the pain easier to bear.'

Sir Pierce was quiet for a moment, thinking.

'My lady said that she was not married when we first talked in the forest, but am I to understand you have no suitor at all in your time?' he said at last. 'You said nobody had been in a position to tell you about your sleep talking?'

'No. There have been people but they are all, well, past.'

'Which is, as I understand it, in the future.'

'Yes,' Maddie said, with a frown. 'But what I mean is, I shall not be hurrying back to any of them when I return. If I return. Of course, we still have no idea if Codoni can help me. Or if she can, whether she *will*.'

'We will ride out as soon as we have eaten,' he replied. It was clear he was trying to hide it but she didn't miss the hollow note in his voice. 'These suitors, in your past, you did with them what you have done with me?'

Maddie, sensing this might be a sensitive subject for a medieval man, stroked Sir Pierce's beard. 'I had sex with them if that's what you mean, otherwise I would not have been in a position to tutor you in the first place. But those experiences were never... satisfying. You... well besides being utterly beautiful, you seem to have a way of knowing just what to say to me.'

'I don't know where those words came from,' he said, a slight blush rising in his cheeks. 'I have never spoken to a woman thus.'

'And as a final lesson, let me advise you not to do so unless the lady makes it clear that she is willing to hear it,' Maddie said with a chuckle. 'I can't think that kind of dirty talk would go down particularly well with noble women of the 16th Century... But, why your sudden interest in my previous partners?'

'I only wondered if you had a suitor in your time as I could not imagine a woman such as yourself not being betrothed. But now it makes sense. None of the suitors in your time are worthy of you.'

Maddie couldn't help but laugh at that idea. 'Oh, I love you for saying that,' she said, before she could stop herself. And then, on realising the words that had slipped out, quickly moved the conversation on. 'What I mean is, I don't think the men of my time think me anything special. Certainly I've never inspired quite the response in them that I've inspired in you.'

'Then they are very foolish.'

'Well, that we can agree on. The last one left me six months ago. Said I was too focused on caring for my mother, and not paying enough attention to him.'

Sir Pierce's whole face darkened. 'And what was he doing to help you and your mother?'

'Absolutely nothing,' said Maddie. 'He wasn't the most giving of individuals. Seems to be a bit of a theme with the suitors I've known, if I'm honest.'

Pierce ran a hand through her hair. 'Promise me something.'

'What would that be?'

'When you return to your time, don't settle for a man who is unworthy of you. You deserve a man who cherishes you. I have known you less than two days and can see that. Promise me you will do this?'

'After meeting you, I fear no man will ever seem worthy again,' she said with a soft smile. 'But yes, I promise.'

A knock at the door startled them both. 'Madame Coustance?' said the chambermaid who had attended to Maddie's needs the night before.

'She cannot see me in here!' Sir Pierce hissed.

'I am indecent just now, my apologies,' Maddie called. 'Could you return in a little while?'

'Yes, Madame Coustance,' said the maid.

'I must away,' said Pierce, grabbing her face and kissing her before leaping to his feet and pulling on his breeches. 'If people are up and see me leaving your chamber, it would not reflect well on you.'

'Not a matter that concerns me too much when I will likely be gone before sundown.'

'As you say, we do not know that the witch Codoni can return you to your time. If she cannot, I will not have people whispering about you.'

Maddie wondered, just for a moment, if Pierce hoped Codoni would not be able to help her, but there wasn't time to analyse his words right now as he was heading for her door.

'Wait, how shall I find you again?' she whispered, wrapping a blanket around her body toga-style and trotting after him in a rather undignified manner.

'I shall join you at breakfast and explain to Sir Richard that I must escort you to the edge of the forest where you will continue your journey north. We should be with the witch Codoni before the afternoon is out.'

'Very well,' she said, 'I shall see you at breakfast, then.'

Pierce, now fully dressed, paused to give her one last look. He reached out a hand and brushed her cheek. 'You are quite beautiful in the mornings, my lady.'

Before she could respond, he had opened the door ajar to check for anyone watching and, the coast being clear, dashed out before anyone could witness his departure.

Pushing the door closed behind him, Maddie tried to ignore the churning in her stomach. When she had first asked Pierce to take her to the Codoni residence, getting back to the 21st Century had been her only desire. Now however, the promise of seeing home again was much diminished by the thought of the tenderly rugged knight she would leave behind.

CHAPTER EIGHTEEN

With just a moment's hesitation, Sir Pierce knocked on the door belonging to the witch Codoni. She lived on the edge of the forest in a rickety old cabin that was better described as a hovel than a home. Though he had heard tall tales of the meddlesome spells and hexes she had cast, he had never had any direct dealings with the woman herself.

After a moment, the door opened and a white-haired woman, bent with age, appeared. She looked first at Maddie and then at Pierce before speaking. 'You are three days early.'

He looked at Maddie, perturbed by the woman's manner and saw that her expression was equally cautious.

'Nevermind three days,' Maddie said with more authority than he had expected of her. 'I'm almost five hundred years early, and by the sound of things, you've got something to do with that.'

'I may have sensed something in the ether,' said the witch Codoni. 'But it seems to me that you're right where you're supposed to be.'

'I'm supposed to be in the future. Long into the future,' said Maddie, firmly. The old woman had quite an irritating manner; given all that was at stake, Sir Pierce thought Maddie's patience nothing short of astonishing.

'No, that is when you were *born*. Where we're born and where we're supposed to be are sometimes two very different matters entirely.'

'I need you to send me back,' said Maddie.

'Back?' the witch Codoni's eyes widened and she pointed a withered finger at Sir Pierce. 'Are you sure you want to go back, given all you've experienced with this man here?'

'How do you know about…' Sir Pierce began, but Maddie held up a hand to silence him.

'It's not about what I want. My mother is very sick. Possibly dying. And I'm the only family she has. I have to go back. I cannot leave her to die alone.'

The witch Codoni considered Maddie's words for a moment.

'I did not foresee such a predicament,' the witch said, musing. 'Still I suppose the powers that be must have their reasons for presenting this choice. I can send you back if that is what you truly want, but the spell in question requires a flower from the forest. One you will have to go searching for.'

'What is the flower?' Maddie asked.

'Myrtle,' the witch Codoni replied. 'It is a white flower. Bring me the myrtle and I will do your bidding and send you back to your time. If that is truly where you think your path lies.'

Slowly, Maddie looked at Sir Pierce, as though weighing up her decision to leave. Had he done enough to show her that if she wanted a home in his arms he would gladly grant her one? All the way through their ride across the forest, Sir Pierce had held her close before him in the saddle, cradling her as if she were his most prized possession. He had kissed her forehead, nibbled playfully at her ears, caressed the curve of her breasts and she in return had leaned back against his chest, stroked his beard, and laced her fingers with his.

And then there had been that comment while they lay in bed that morning. She had let slip that she loved him. Lord, those words had been enough to make his head spin. His heart swelled to hear them. But she had then quickly changed the subject and thus he could not be sure if this was something everyone from her time said to each other quite casually, or if the words had more weight than her manner had suggested.

When she gave the witch Codoni her response however, he had his answer.

'Yes,' she said. 'My path is in service of my mother. I must get back to her as quickly as I can.'

CHAPTER NINETEEN

'ere it is,' said Sir Pierce, crouching near some long grasses and reaching into the forest foliage to pick what Maddie assumed to be the myrtle flower. At his discovery, his voice was as flatly disappointed as she felt.

What a terrible choice.

To leave behind the only man she had ever truly surrendered to or face never seeing her beloved mother again. Maddie knew if her mother were apprised of this situation, she would insist Maddie prioritise her own happiness. But she could not do that. She could not leave her mother to face her recovery, or decline, alone.

'Thank you,' she said, accepting the white flower from Sir Pierce's big, strong hands as he stood and offered it to her. She once again looked into the strange glimmer of his deep brown eyes, trying to commit his rugged beauty to memory. She had that precious photograph of the two of them from when they had first met. But she had no idea if that photo might be erased through the process of time travel. In truth, she still considered that she may yet wake up in a hospital bed from a coma or even worse, never wake up at all.

'I've never had a relationship end quite like this before,' she said, trying hard to keep her tone light even though the decision to leave behind a man like Sir Pierce weighed heavy.

'You mean you never before left a man to travel back through time? Lady, you have not lived your life to the fullest.' The sunlight flickering through the trees made his eyes shine even brighter in amusement.

In spite of the heartbreaking goodbye that awaited, Maddie smirked and made a show of looking surprised. 'Why Sir Pierce, you made a joke. An intentional joke.'

'I have been rather too preoccupied in the last day or two to be making merry, my lady.'

'Yes, I suppose being accused of murder can rather put a dampener on a person's sense of humour. But, no, what I meant was that I have never had a relationship end on such good terms. Which given that I'm about to say goodbye to you to travel five hundred years into the future doesn't exactly say a lot for the way my previous liaisons have ended.'

'I think this may also be the most cordial parting I have ever had with a woman,' said Sir Pierce, a quiet astonishment in his voice as though he was only realising this fact just now. He took another step towards her so that they were now but inches apart. 'Is it madness that I wish I could travel back with you?'

She wondered for a moment if he were making a joke but when she looked at him again his expression was completely sincere. The lines on his face tight with anticipation. His jaw set as he awaited his answer.

'I'm afraid it is, as mad as me desperately wishing there was a way of plucking a man out of his own time and planting him in my own. But I suppose we must just be thankful for the time we've shared together. And remember that we have just met. We haven't really had the time to properly get to know each other.'

Sir Pierce looked at Maddie for a long moment. 'I do not know how things work in your time. But here two days of knowing a lady as intimately as I have come to know you is time enough. Knights are never very long for this world. In fact at three and thirty years of age I am already older than most knights. Most of us die before our third decade. Take too long to decide on a woman and you may be dead before you can marry her.'

'How romantic,' Maddie said with a chuckle, rolling the r on 'romantic' for effect.

'I fear, my lady, that you are purposefully misunderstanding me.'

'Would I?'

'Yes.' Sir Pierce said, pulling her into his body.

She took a deep breath and savoured the feeling of his hard muscles pressed against her. 'I couldn't ask you to leave your world behind for me,' she whispered.

'You didn't ask me. I offered myself to you. And lady, what world? All those I have ever truly loved in this world have long since left it. Have you not understood, in the time we have spent together, that there is nothing in my world but fighting and death? There hasn't been for many years. You are the first light and warmth I have known in as long as I can remember.'

Maddie reached a hand up to his cheek and stroked his beard. 'Oh Pierce, I feel the same about you. Truly, I do. But that is a huge amount of pressure to pile on a relationship. My time is very different to this one in too many ways to explain. What if it didn't work out and then you were stuck in the 21st Century?'

'Why would our union not work out?'

Looking up at him, she privately admitted that, in that moment, she couldn't think of a single reason why it wouldn't. He had made it clear that he would not run off when the going got tough like James had. He had told her that she deserved to be cherished. She assumed, since he was willing to travel five hundred years through time with her, that he wanted to be the one to do that. 'I don't know why it wouldn't,' she answered honestly, it's just, it never has worked out before.'

'That is because, my lady, you have never before given yourself to me. I heard how the witch Codoni spoke to you. She was not expecting you to go back to your time once we had met. Seemingly, her future relation sent you through time into my path. And I cannot believe that is coincidence. Of course, if you don't wish to be with me, that is another matter. You need only say.'

The second that sentence left his mouth, Maddie put a hand over his lips. 'Please do not say that, don't even think it. I've never wanted anyone more than I've wanted you.'

Sir Pierce smiled at this and kissed his way from Maddie's freckled nose all the way to her ear lobe before whispering: 'Then, my lady, no matter what the century, you shall have me.'

CHAPTER TWENTY

'What do you mean, it can't be done?' Lady Madelyn said. Though her voice was in competition with the hissing and bubbling of the potion the witch Codoni was brewing over the fire, the incredulous nature of his lady's tone was still most noticeable. 'You're sending me anyway, surely it's possible to send Pierce too?'

'It's not so much that I'm certain it cannot be done,' the witch Codoni clarified. 'It's just that neither myself, nor any of my ancestors, have ever attempted such a feat before. Magic can be precarious and isn't to be toyed with. I cannot entirely say what the outcome could be. By sending two people instead of one, there might be some unintended consequences that we cannot foresee.'

'Such as?' Sir Pierce pushed. He wasn't entirely sure the old crone could send either him or Lady Madelyn through time, but it was perhaps wise to know what could go wrong if her attempt went awry. Besides, he hadn't planned on entering Codoni's hovel and the more there was to distract him from the strange piles of bird feathers in every corner, and the peculiar collection of bottles lining one of the walls, the better.

'Simply because I send you at the same moment, does not mean you are guaranteed to land in the same time. You may land centuries apart. Or your bodies might get mixed up on the journey and you might return to the 21st Century as half yourself and half the other person.'

Sir Pierce paused. 'You mean, half of my body might be fused with half of Lady Madelyn's?'

The witch Codoni shrugged. 'It is just a theory.'

'Which half?' Sir Pierce asked, before he received a swift but playful shove from Lady Madelyn.

'I don't think having half of each other's body is a desirable scenario in any case,' she said.

'Speak for yourself,' Sir Pierce replied with a rakish grin.

Madelyn shook her head at him. 'I don't think we should take any unnecessary risks. Can't you send us both separately?'

The witch Codoni stared at Madelyn for a long moment, her expression nothing short of scathing, before she deigned to reply. 'Do you think we can perform this magic every week? Once in a generation we are able to cast this spell. On a person who we believe deserving of a greater destiny than they've been allotted in their own time. You are lucky I haven't yet used the spell. Otherwise I would not be able to send you back.'

'So that means... for some reason Madame Codoni thought me deserving,' Lady Madelyn said.

'For some reason? For some reason?' the witch Codoni repeated in an excitable manner. 'You were but an hour ago willing to leave the man you were destined to meet to care for your mother. Few would even consider such a sacrifice. There is no question that you are deserving.'

A slight blush rose in Lady Madelyn's cheeks at the witch's praise. She clearly was not aware of just how bright the goodness in her shone. As he surveyed her, Sir Pierce made a private vow to rectify that at the first possible opportunity. Assuming he survived the process of time travel.

'But you said I was three days early, so you were expecting us,' Lady Madelyn said, moving the conversation on from her finer qualities. 'You knew I would want to travel back.'

'I was expecting you to have sought me out to thank me for your happy ever after. It wasn't I who cast the spell that brought you here, of course, but I could have written a letter to future generations of the family expressing your gratitude for our help in finding the man of your dreams.'

'Oh,' Maddie said, looking suitably sheepish. 'Sorry about that. I never meant to seem ungrateful. I couldn't be more glad to have found Sir Pierce and I wouldn't ask to go back to my time if it weren't an emergency.'

The witch Codoni let out a gentle sigh. 'I know that, child. The broth is almost ready however, so you must make your choice soon. If you choose to travel together, beware that I cannot guarantee that you will find each other again.'

Lady Madelyn looked at Sir Pierce and pursed her lips. 'The risks are too great, Pierce.'

Drawing closer to her, he took her soft hands in his. 'I think not, my lady. I have risked far greater danger for much lesser reward. And although I am concerned that any adverse outcome might affect you, I believe this to be a matter of faith. I do not believe that powers greater than ourselves would have brought us together, only to tear us apart. I refuse to believe it, in fact. I have every faith that if we do this together, we will live together from this day forward.'

'That's a lot to take on faith,' Lady Madelyn said, a wavering note in her voice.

Leaning downward, he touched his forehead against hers. 'It is no more to take on faith than that the lady who magically appears in the path of your horse is from some unknown future,' he said, his voice soft, soothing.

'I… suppose.'

'Look into my eyes,' he said, 'and tell me you do not believe it.'

She did as instructed and, as her twinkling green eyes met with his, and a small smile crept across her lips, he knew she felt as he did.

'Very well, my lord,' she said. 'We will take the chance.'

But a few moments later, the witch Codoni returned from the pot with two silver goblets. 'It's still a little bit hot so be careful. You must drink it all down at the same time and, if you want to maximise the chances of you both turning up in the same century, I would recommend holding hands.'

Sir Pierce accepted the goblet from the witch Codoni and Lady Madelyn did the same. Without hesitation, he laced his fingers through hers, gripping her hand tight so the greater powers might suffer no confusion over the fact that he desired to stay at this woman's side for as long as it was humanly possible.

Nodding at each other, they drank the potion down in synchrony before handing the goblets back to their host.

An awkward moment followed where nothing happened. Lady Madelyn looked at him, he looked at Lady Madelyn and then they both looked at the witch Codoni.

'Have you been fooling us all this time, Codoni?' he said. But no sooner had he said the words than the room began to spin. As their surroundings blurred, he tightened his grip on Lady Madelyn's hand and felt her do the same.

And then he fell. Or at least, he thought he was falling. But he could not be sure for all around him was blackness. As though he was suspended in some great unknown. He felt Lady Madelyn's hand in his own but he could not see her. He could not see anything. Or hear anything for that matter.

Everything about him had become a void.

CHAPTER TWENTY ONE

'It's alright,' said an unfamiliar voice. 'I think she's coming around.'

For a moment, Maddie wondered who the voice was talking about, but as her eyes fluttered open and she looked up to see a circle of concerned faces, she realised they had been talking about her.

'You alright, love?' said a woman with purple hair. 'You had a nasty fall.'

'A fall?' Maddie said, blinking. And then she remembered. The conference hall. The potion she'd drunk. The way she'd tumbled to the ground.

Had that been all it was? All *he* was? A side-effect of concussion? At that thought she felt the urge to burst into tears but pride helped her to just about hold them back.

'I'm perfectly fine,' she lied, taking the hand of one of the gawking strangers to help herself up. 'I've..I've just been working too hard lately.'

'I think you'd better go to the medical bay,' the woman with purple hair pushed.

'Yes, I'll do just that,' Maddie said, though the only thing she planned to do was go straight home and cry under her duvet for hours.

Once reassured, the small crowd dispersed and Maddie leaned on a nearby table, trying to catch her breath. She glanced over at where Madame Codoni's wagon had stood, wondering if perhaps she would have some answers. But the wagon, and Madame Codoni were gone.

Had she really imagined the whole thing? Oh no, the emptiness that filled her at that thought was too great to bear. All of this time, she had been so focused on caring for her mother without anyone to care for her. And then she'd met Pierce. He had saved her life from the arrows and swords hurtling in her direction, yes. But he had also cared for her in more subtle ways. Holding her, caressing her, listening to her. Such simple gestures and yet they had been completely lacking in all of her other relationships. And now he was gone and all she had left of him were memories.

It was then she remembered the photograph she'd taken of herself and Sir Pierce. Hastily, she opened her satchel and pulled out her phone. As she stared at the first photograph in her camera roll, a tear slid down her cheek.

There he was. Her rugged knight. Looking utterly bemused as she pointed a contraption at him that was completely beyond his realm of experience.

So it was real. But he was not here with her. Was he? She bit her lip, glancing around again, just in case, but he was nowhere among the meandering crowd. Which meant he must be lost in time somewhere, just as Madame Codoni's ancestor had feared. The thought of him being stranded in a place unfamiliar and unknown was more than she could bear. She should have been firmer with him. He had risked his very life for her and now, not only would she never see him again, he may meet some terrible end on account of her.

She looked again at the photograph. What kind of cruel trick had the universe played here? What was she supposed to do now? Simply be grateful that she had spent any time at all in the arms of the man that she loved? With some perspective, maybe she would be able to do that. Just then however grief filled her so entirely it was almost impossible to breathe.

Studying the photograph again, she concentrated on those entrancing brown eyes. And as she did so, she thought she heard his voice. She stopped breathing and listened.

'Madam! Unhand me at once,' the voice was saying. 'I am perfectly aware of what a selfie is but I have other, more pressing, matters to attend to.'

Maddie frowned. Her whole body was rigid. She barely dared to blink in case doing so sent some strange ripple through the space time continuum that might cause Sir Pierce to vanish. Or in case closer examination of the voice she had heard revealed it to be nothing more than the wishful delusions of a silly woman in grief who had hit her head too hard when she had fallen.

Still, she couldn't stay still forever.

Bracing herself for the brutal and inevitable dashing of hope, she turned to where the voice seemed to be coming from. She could not quite believe what she saw.

Her knight!

He was being accosted by several women, all trying to take photographs with him. It appeared they thought him one of the attractions at the convention. Given that he was dressed head to toe in his mail, Maddie could not much blame them for that assumption.

On knowing that he was here, that they had made it, Maddie felt a soothing warmth spread right through her. The kind of feeling a person feels once, perhaps twice in their lifetime if they're lucky. The feeling that someone far more important than you is looking after your greater happiness. What other explanation was there for this strange twist of events?

Without wasting another moment on the whys or wherefores, Maddie sped towards the man she had fallen through time for.

'Pierce!' she called, and at the sound of her voice he turned to see her making her way through the crowds.

Swatting away the mobile phones pointed in his direction, Sir Pierce strode towards her. In seconds they were in each other's arms, laughing with relief. Several onlookers gathered round clearly suspecting them to be part of the day's entertainment. Maddie did not care what they thought or who was watching. All she could see was him.

'Pierce,' she whispered as he covered her mouth with his own and delivered a deep, hot kiss. She clawed at the cool metal of his mail, desperate to find any way to hold onto him in case he was somehow ripped from the present, just as she had been.

'I thought we had been separated,' he said, when at last their lips parted.

'Me too. I thought I'd lost you,' she said, unable to stop a single tear of relief falling as she truly digested the fact that this wasn't the case.

Pierce brushed the tear away with the back of his hand. 'Well, just in case there is a danger of that, I think it best that we hold each other very tight from this day forward.'

'Seems like very sound advice,' Maddie replied, cupping his perfect face in his hands while raising a cheeky eyebrow at him. 'I do appreciate a man with a tight grip.'

'So I remember,' he murmured, the rush of his voice in her ears leaving her breathless. 'Don't worry, my lady, I promise that, as long as there is strength in these arms, I will never let you go.'

Want to receive advanced discounted copies of Helen's other titles?
Please visit: helencoxbooks.com/mailinglist

If you enjoyed this story please consider leaving a review.

ABOUT THE AUTHOR

Helen Cox is a Yorkshire-born novelist and poet. After completing her MA in creative writing at the University of York St. John Helen wrote for a range of publications, edited her own independent film magazine for five years and penned three non-fiction books. Her first two novels were published by HarperCollins in 2016. She currently lives by the sea in Sunderland where she writes poetry, romance novellas, and The Kitt Hartley series alongside hosting The Poetrygram podcast.

http://helencoxbooks.com

CPSIA information can be obtained
at www.ICGtesting.com
Printed in the USA
LVHW112308190721
693163LV00005B/234/J

9 781914 238017